The Better To Eat You With

A Fairytale Romance
by Serenity Sky

Published in 2021 by
Ballads & Bards Bookhouse

Ballads & Bards Bookhouse
Wonnarua Country
Suite 92, Ground Floor
1 Market Street,
Newcastle, NSW 2300
AUSTRALIA
www.balladsandbardsbookhouse.com

A catalogue record of this work is available from the National Library of Australia

The Better To Eat You With: A Fairytale Romance
ISBN: 978 0 6451408 2 8 (paperback)

10 9 8 7 6 5 4 3 2 1

Cover Design
Nabin Karna

Text Design
Istvan Szabo

Editor
Dr Danny Decillis

Printed by Ingram Spark, an Ingram Industries company, and Kindle Direct Printing, an Amazon company.

Ballads & Bards Bookhouse acknowledges the Traditional Owners of the country on which we work, the Wonnarua and Awabakal nations, and recognises their continuing connection to their land, waters and culture. We pay respects to their Elders past, present and emerging.

Dedicated to N,
He just HAD to read it first...

TABLE OF CONTENTS

Prologue.. 1

Chapter One.. 3

Chapter Two 12

Chapter Three 19

Chapter Four.. 29

Chapter Five... 37

Chapter Six 45

Chapter Seven 60

Chapter Eight 72

Chapter Nine... 77

Chapter Ten 86

Chapter Eleven 92

Chapter Twelve 101

Chapter Thirteen 113

Chapter Fourteen.......................................125

Chapter Fifteen...134

Chapter Sixteen 145

Chapter Seventeen 157

Chapter Eighteen.......................................166

PROLOGUE

Scarlett was running. As she dodged between the trees, her cloak flying behind her, she heard the blood pounding in her ears as twigs and branches snapped under her feet. She cried out in fear as there was a long howl behind her. It was closer than before. Scarlett didn't have a lot of time to get out of the woods before she was caught. She could have sworn she hadn't gone this far into the trees. It should not be taking this long to get back out. Had she taken a wrong turn?

Scarlett pushed on as fast as her feet could carry her, her chest heaving as she desperately breathed in the icy night air. She knew she could not last much longer, which proved irrelevant when she ran into a clearing and suddenly came across a massive wall of boulders blocking her way.

It was not possible. She had roamed these woods all her life. There had never been *anything* in it like what she was seeing now. Where had it come from?

Scarlett did not have time to consider the thought, before the clearing filled with a low, deep growling. She spun around and found herself face to face with a monster sized wolf; its long, thick fur the darkest russet red. Scarlett screamed and fell back as it leapt at her, jaws dripping. She hit the ground and started scrambling backwards, but her cloak got caught on a branch.

The wolf was upon her in two strides, and as its paws landed on her shoulders, the fur melted away to reveal scarred, pale skin and thick locks of the same dark red hair. It was a man; a man with deep green eyes and black, talon-like fingernails. His canine teeth came down over his bottom lip… and he was completely naked.

Scarlett's heartbeat was coming in short flutters now. She felt herself grow slick. The shock had left her frozen before his talons raked across her chest, tearing away her blood red cloak, leaving her as bare as he. "You are human!" she finally choked.

"I… am *hunger*," he growled, his broad chest rumbling with the depth of his voice, before he raised Scarlett's hips and plunged deep inside her.

Her eyes snapped shut at the impact. She let out a strangled gasp and when she opened her eyes again, she was lying in her own bed, the cool night air drifting in through the open window and the mattress damp with her wetness, as she had found herself so many times before.

1-SCARLETT

Scarlett had lived in the Boque Village her entire life, and for half of that life she had been plagued by nightmares. They followed her into her waking moments, reminding her of what she had suffered even when the townsfolk were not around to do it themselves with their looks of pity, awe, and commiseration.

Only recently had they taken a turn she had never experienced before. She usually woke up before the wolf caught her, her heart still racing and her bed just as moist, but with sweat. Recently however, her dreams had turned carnal in nature, with the wolf catching and devouring her in different ways almost every night. She remembered every single one, too.

As she strolled through Boque on her way to the bakery, she caught numerous glances from the village people. "How are you today, Dear?" Mistress Quinn asked.

"I am very well, thank you, Mistress Quinn."

"Holding up alright, Scar?" Bobby the stable boy at Winston Farms called out from across the square. Scarlett smiled and waved in reply. "I am just fine, Bobby."

"My condolences, Girl," an elderly man called Blue said to her as he sat out the front of the blacksmiths. "As if you have not been through enough already."

"Thank you, Sir," Scarlett answered politely. This was the way in Boque. She would go to the town square to collect the things her family needed and trade her herbs in return in between market days. On her way people would stop her multiple times to fuss over her. It was getting rather tedious after all these years.

When Scarlett was ten years old, she had fallen afoul of the wolf plague. Her grandmother had been rather ill and her mother was stuck at the family farm making sure they could make ends meet while her father was away on patrol, hunting the pack that had started targeting the village. Her mother had asked her to take some supplies to her grandmother's and help her with anything she might need around the house and garden, but she had stressed to Scarlett the importance of remaining inside once the sun went down and not attempting to return until the sun had well and truly risen the next day.

Scarlett had readily agreed and insisted she understood, eager to see her grandmother and help her, but also to get away from the monotonous life of the farm that was becoming drearier and more miserable every day. However... Scarlett was also ten, and at that age, was an easily distractible girl. She passed others on the outskirts of the trees who she dallied with; adults who questioned where she was off to and children who asked her to play for just a few minutes.

These encounters slowly dissipated the deeper she went into the woods, for only her grandmother lived so far in, but when she neared the main fork in the path, she heard a deep voice coming through the trees. It was odd because the only other people who travelled this far into the woods were the woodcutters and they were usually gone before the heat of the day had settled in during the summer, or the work became too arduous.

She had forgotten at the time that the woodcutters had started taking shifts roaming the forests in an attempt to find the wolves den while they slept during the day. "Sir?" Scarlett had called back cautiously, peering through the trees.

"What is a pretty little thing like you doing out here?" the voice had asked softly.

"I need to take supplies to my grandmother," Scarlett had answered proudly, holding herself tall. "She is very sick and cannot get out of bed, you see."

"Is that so? And she lives all the way out here? *Alone?*"

"Yes, Sir; just down the left hand fork, but I know where I am going," she had insisted. "I come here all the time." It was the way of Boque; to keep an eye on all around you and to check in with your neighbours regularly. When Scarlett heard the voice talking to her, she assumed it was one of the late working woodcutters, finally remembering the wolf den search was still underway.

"That is very kind of you," the sickly sweet voice continued. "You know what sick people find *particularly* pleasing?"

"What's that?" Scarlett had asked eagerly.

"Flowers!"

"Flowers?"

"Yes, Child, such as the ones growing around the trees here. Night lights and bluebells. People find great cheer in them, I have noticed."

"What a wonderful idea! Thank you!" Scarlett had called out gratefully, before setting out to collect as many different wildflowers as she could find. She picked flowers and fruits and as she passed them, amassing a collection for her to carry to her ailing grandmother. With a full basket she had rejoined the path and continued on to the cottage in the woods.

When she had arrived, calling out as she climbed the stairs, her grandmother hadn't answered. Scarlett had let herself in, finding her grandmother already asleep in bed, the blankets close up near her face. She quickly and quietly set about pulling the flowers and supplies from her basket. When her work was complete and the flowers were sat daintily around the kitchen and living areas around the fireplace, she had found herself unbearably tired from the journey, so she had curled up with several blankets in the front of the fire and gone to sleep.

When Scarlett awoke just before sunrise, she went to wake her grandmother for her morning tea, her ten year old eyes not noticing the torn blankets on the floor, or the trickles of blood splattered on the walls, or even the upended table by the trunk that sat at the end of her grandmother's bed.

Her grandmother wasn't in the bed. When she drew back the covers, there was a chilling snarl and she was knocked to the ground by a mountain of dark grey fur. Just as its jaws locked on her forearm, there was an almighty crash and the door flew open. In a single swing of his axe, a Boque woodcutter had felled the beast and saved Scarlett and her grandmother, who was found clawed and bleeding on the other side of the bed.

Scarlett's father never returned from that patrol. Her mother had lost her husband and very nearly her mother and daughter all in one night. Scarlett had relived the memory of the attack almost every moment of her life in the years that followed. Thoughts of it would plague her throughout the day and nightmares would wake her at night.

Her mother, Ingrid, had insisted Scarlett's grandmother move in with them following the attack, forcing her to give up the cabin in the woods for the safety of Boque. Ingrid Black was a proud woman, never accepting help from anyone after the death of her husband, adamant that she could do everything herself. Once her mother and daughter had become the potential second and third losses of her family to the wolf plague, she had committed herself to ending it for good. Every single day from that to this, she had trained.

She utilised the skills of the woodcutter, who gladly taught her how to use his tools for defence. She then turned to other forms of weaponry. Swords, daggers, the bow; she learnt them all. The farm had fallen almost completely into Scarlett's hands as her mother started a lucrative side business in hunting.

She started with the wolf that had attacked Scarlett and her mother, returning to the cabin in the woods one final time to collect the pelt. Using it, she tracked the others; or rather, she used it to allow them to track *her*. One by one she hunted every single wolf in the area. Sometimes other hunters and woodcutters joined her, but most did not want the company of a woman and so kept their distance from her endeavour. They considered her to be reckless and courting disaster to be out hunting the beasts and as such, they wanted no part of it.

Every trip she would return with the heads of her kill, which were placed on spears that ran along the fence line of the farm. When the final wolf den had been discovered and eradicated, Ingrid had returned home from the final hunt with the last of the heads to find the people of the town were all there to greet her. Their opinions had changed greatly. Where once they chided her, they now cheered her name for the great deed she had done for the safety of Boque, and whenever they found themselves prey to vermin, be it pest or predator, they came to Ingrid for help, and so her business grew.

Scarlett ran the farm now, with the help of attendants paid for by her mother. There was a multitude of herb gardens which she tended to herself, as well as a fruit orchard, a vegetable patch and a large hen house. It was a small enterprise by farming standards, but with her mother's business doing so well, there was no need to expand when Boque already had everything it needed, and Scarlett would not be able to handle any more responsibilities even if it did not.

Ten years had passed since that fateful day. The scar on her arm was still disfiguring but had faded over the years. What hadn't faded were the memories. Not only was Scarlett famous for being one of only two who had ever survived a wolf attack during the plague, but she was the trigger that led her mother to become one of the town's most respected and well-known citizens. This meant that wherever she went, people knew her.

Even after she grew out of her red woollen cloak her grandmother had made her as a child, her long dark locks, her scar and her very presence were enough to draw attention. She had actually come across another cloak, packed away deep in her grandmother's trunk at the foot of her bed at the farm only a few months past. She had shuddered in horror and dropped it back in; slamming the lid closed like it housed a poisonous snake and had not gone near the trunk again.

But, despite not wearing the infamous cloak, and even when she would actively avoid the topic, the people of Boque would always bring up the attack, bringing with it the memories, pulling them back to the forefront of her mind. This made her feel like she was living in a never ending time loop, where no matter how much older she became, a child she forever remained.

2-SCARLETT

Scarlett entered the bakery, one of her least favourite places in all of Boque. It was there that the supplies for her grandmother had been collected and so carefully placed into her basket. It was a constant reminder of what had happened, and on the off chance she was in such a rush to return to the farm that she was *not* thinking about it, Jacques and Rohan, the bakery giants; hulking bears of men; were sure to remind her. Tall, robust, and cheerful, they were wonderfully kind souls, but Scarlett found them incredibly draining when she had to hear them fuss over her the way they did, or worse, insist that their son Keenen was the only possible match for her in all the town and surrounding village.

Standing behind the bakery counter, kneading dough, was Keenen himself. He was the exact opposite of his fathers. Adopted as a young child when the first wave of the wolf plague took his birth parents, he had black hair and dark eyes, while Jacques and Rohan were a sandy brown and a white blonde. He was also almost a foot shorter and much thinner than they. Jacques and Rohan would often joke that he must keep everything in his big toe, because no matter how much of their goods he ate, which was a lot, he never got any bigger.

He was not just the opposite in looks, but also demeanour. Jacques and Rohan were kind and caring; Keenen was arrogant and pompous. Jacques and Rohan led Scarlett to feel warm and safe; Keenen made her feel uncomfortable and shaky. The bakery providing such a vital staple meant it was as wealthy as Scarlett's farm and just as highly respected. It had been a long standing assumption that she and Keenen would marry one day, but the idea turned her stomach.

"Morning Scarlett," he smiled, pretention dripping from his lips.

"Keenen," Scarlett exhaled heavily.

"Whatever can the bakery provide for you today?" he went on, placing the dough into its signature knot on the firing tray and sliding it into the fireplace oven, closing its thick metal door to seal in the heat. He turned back to her, a smirk playing at the corner of his mouth coyly. "You know you are always welcome to… *whatever* you like here," he said, taking a step forward with his arms out encouragingly.

"Thank you, Keenen," Scarlett replied briskly, her face reddening. "I am just here for the trade." She pulled the herb bundles out of her basket and placed them on the counter, refusing to meet his eyes.

Keenen nodded and selected several loaves and cakes from the shelves, wrapping them infuriatingly slowly. "You know," he began, gazing Scarlett up and down longingly as he came around the counter. "You should join the festivals and banquets that are thrown here in town. You don't need to hide yourself away out on that farm of yours."

"I don't believe I do," Scarlett said, her hand coming to her throat protectively. "I simply choose what company I keep."

"Well, I hope I am considered among the party!" he grinned, moving closer. "I most definitely have *more* to offer you than most." He was standing very close to her, the breads forgotten.

Scarlett's face grew hotter as she felt his warm breath on the side of her face, and the bulge in his pants pressed against her mound. She shook herself slightly and stepped back. "No thank you, Keenen; the bread will suffice." She quickly grabbed the goods and side stepped Keenen, flying out the door.

No, she did not like the bakery at all...

Outside in the crisp morning air of winter, Scarlett took a deep breath in an attempt to control the chills running through her body. After a slight shiver, she decided to clear her head with a walk. She headed for the cemetery, the ache between her legs gradually beginning to dissipate. The snap of the cold was a stark contrast to the heat of the bakery, in a number of ways, and it brought Scarlett back to her senses with each step she took.

Despite an unbearable dislike of Keenen, she could not help the impact he had on her. She raised her arms above her head, stretching as a means to clear her head, the throb between her legs lessening to a dull twinge. Keenen was certainly attractive enough, giving rise to many sensations Scarlett fought to keep in check, but his gravitas was so incredibly off putting that the idea of remaining in his company long enough to explore such sensations was torture.

When Scarlett entered the sacred ground where the citizens of Boque were laid to rest, she found herself calmer; her body finally quiet. She sighed at the relief as she made her way down the rows, to the newest ones. There was where she found what she was looking for; only one of two she ever came to see.

HERE LIES ROSA GERTRUDE BLACK
Beloved Mother & Grandmother
Matriarch of the Black Family
DIED AGE 58

Scarlett breathed in deeply and exhaled slowly, remembering her grandmother. Rosa was one of the strongest people she had ever known, but her own mother, Ingrid, clearly showed that her untenable strength ran in the family. Scarlett loved her grandmother deeply, and she still hadn't fully come to terms with the pain of losing her.

After the attack at her cabin, Rosa had come to live with them at the farm, but she had never fully healed from the trauma. Her body had become slower, she developed a spasm in her left side and had needed to walk with a cane ever since. She did not leave the farm for anything, always sending Scarlett on her errands if she needed something.

She spent her days watching Ingrid train, barking orders about her maintaining her form and teaching both she and Scarlett survival skills, such as lighting a fire and making weapons by sharpening stones to act as blades, spears, and arrow heads. Rosa Black was a remarkably innovative and ingenious woman.

She had slowly deteriorated over the years, finally announcing that it was her time to die. Ingrid was adamant that was not going to happen. "Not on my watch, Mother!"

"Well, you cannot watch me forever, can you?" Rosa had snapped stubbornly, and sure enough, three days after her declaration… she was gone.

Her funeral rites had been held the following day. The entire town came to pay their respects, and as such, her tombstone was adorned with the most beautiful carvings, flowers, trinkets, and gifts to send her into the afterlife. There were many people Scarlett had not seen for many years, including the very woodcutter who had saved them both all those years ago; Hector Bloom.

Scarlett had spent a year of her childhood with the woodcutter at the farm after the wolf attack. He had taught her mother how to spar and had given Scarlett her first dagger. Scarlett always felt that Hector had feelings for her mother, but Ingrid was so committed to and focused on her training and the task of wiping out the wolf plague that her disinterest was clear.

Scarlett assumed that was what eventually led him to stop returning, but here he was again; showing solidarity for Rosa, saying goodbye for the last time. He was not alone either.

"Scarlett! Dear girl, how are you?" Hector embraced her warmly.

"Hector! You came," she responded quietly.

"How could I not?" he gave her a final squeeze before releasing her. "Let me look at you! How is your mother?"

"As can be expected, I am afraid," Scarlett answered. "This has unsettled her greatly. I do not know what she will do without Grandmother, but she will not allow anyone to see her in pain. She feels it makes her appear weak."

Hector the woodcutter nodded sadly. "Well, let us make sure she gets through this, shall we?" Scarlett nodded. "Where are my manners!" he suddenly said. "May I present to you, Gabriel... my son."

Their eyes met--hers deep brown, his steely grey--and from that moment both of their lives were different. For Scarlett, that was when the dreams she had each night changed, but for Gabriel, that moment was when he knew the ones he had for his waking life would never be the same.

3-GABRIEL

Gabriel Bloom had known only one life; that of a woodcutter. First, he was a baby, hearing the sounds of his father sharpening the blades of dozens of axes. Then he was a toddler, being given small wooden replicas to play with. After that he was a boy, learning all about the different types of blades and what trees they were used for.

From a youth he had practiced and practiced on younger trees, keeping enough wood for the family fireplace so that his father could sell everything he cut down in the deep woods to the townsfolk who could not collect it themselves, or the richer families who simply did not want to. As many woodcutters acted as patrolmen, many of them were lost during the wolf plague. This left a lot of business for his father and the remaining woodcutters. His father did the best he could to provide.

Now as an adult, Gabriel was trusted to take care of the homestead. He had cultivated a collection of tools almost larger than his father's, each piece lovingly handmade from blade to handle and detailed enough to rival the work of the most skilled blacksmiths.

Gabriel's mother had died in childbirth, and so had not experienced the development of the wolf plague. It was only Hector raising his boy until the third year of attacks, when his sister's husband was killed by one of the roaming packs. Gabriel was seven at the time, and it was then that his Aunt Grace came to live with them. He was with her when Hector started the wolf patrols, he was with her when Hector saved Rosa and Scarlett that day in the woods, and it was there he remained when his father would spend time with Ingrid at the Black family farm.

"Is Father at the farm again, Aunt Grace?" he would ask.

"Oh, you know your father," she would answer dismissively. "He thinks he can get that Ingrid woman to marry him. He is lonely, your father," she sighed.

"So… Ingrid could become my new Mother?" Gabriel had asked earnestly.

"I do not think so, Gabriel," Aunt Grace had said sadly, stroking his hair. "Ingrid seems… rather *opposed* to catching the interest of men."

Gabriel did not understand what that meant, and after a while his father stopped going to the farm and refocused his attention on work. That was when the business really took off. Gabriel was old enough to start working with Hector and after a few years of Ingrid's efforts, it meant being able to sell to other towns and villages who did not have the privilege of the level of safety Boque had now.

Being younger and faster Gabriel did a lot of the travelling to barter for sales and trades, leaving the bulk of the brute strength work to his father. Because of this arrangement Gabriel was rarely in town and when he was, he was in the woods. And so it came to be that it was only when the famous Rosa Black died and he attended her funeral with his father, that he came face to face with Scarlett Black for the first time.

Gabriel stopped breathing. If *this* was the daughter, then it was blatantly obvious why the mother, Ingrid, had garnered so much of his father's attention. Gabriel found himself unable to speak, so he bowed slightly in greeting and stayed silent. He felt a tug deep in his stomach and his mouth was suddenly dry. Scarlett peered back at him, her face inscrutable, but tense. Gabriel forced himself to blink, breaking the connection.

"I am going to talk to your mother, convince her to let us fix you all dinner soon," Hector's voice cut through the tension.

Scarlett paused for a split second before finding her voice. "Y-yes, Hector, I am sure that would be lovely. Thank you." Gabriel pulled himself together enough to bow slightly in goodbye before following his father over to where Ingrid sat on one of the concrete benches that ran along the side of the tombstones, glancing back at Scarlett as he went.

When the funeral rites had been completed and the ceremony was brought to an end, the entire town accompanied the Black family back to their farm, as was tradition. Food was laid out, black lace covered the mirrors and the candles were all burning low.

The farmhouse was bigger than Gabriel and Hector's, and was tended to by several maids. After paying his respects to Ingrid for her loss, Gabriel collected a plate of food and went to sit outside by the barn. It was a calm and quiet day; the right kind of day to be seeing someone off for the last time.

While he ate his food, distracted by his thoughts, he did not realise he was being watched. "Would you like some company?" a quiet voice asked.

Scarlett.

Gabriel choked on his food. "O-of course!" he finally managed to say.

Scarlett took a seat on the grass next to him, leaning back against the wall of the barn. "I never knew Hector had a son," she said.

"All the times he came here and I was not mentioned at all?" Gabriel was hurt by the idea. Had his father really dismissed him so during his failed courtship of Ingrid Black?

"It is possible you were," Scarlett said thoughtfully. Gabriel could not stop watching her; the way she moved, how she sat and spoke, the way she played with her fingertips as she thought. His eyes drifted to the nape of her neck as she drew the curtain of dark hair together over one shoulder.

"Hector was not around me a lot; he was just *here*," Scarlett explained. "It was only after he stopped visiting us here and I had grown older that Mother began to train me in the things he had taught her and I started working on the farm beyond the herb garden. I am sure he would have mentioned you to Mother while they were training. Do you know why he suddenly stopped coming?"

"My aunt thinks he was attempting to court your mother," Gabriel told her. "And stopped visiting the farm when he realised it was never going to work." At this, Scarlett burst out laughing; a delicious peal of brightness on what was a dark and sombre day. She quickly caught herself, stifling her laughter. "What is so funny?" he asked, smiling at the sound.

"My mother does not keep the company of men unless they are paying her for her services, and even then, she sticks to hunting," Scarlett smiled broadly.

"Yes, my aunt said as much," Gabriel nodded. "How are you after the funeral? The rites were beautiful," he said, changing the subject.

Scarlett sighed heavily, as though the weight of the world was settling on her. "I wish people would stop asking me that."

"I am sorry," Gabriel said quickly. "I just-"

"-No! It is not your fault," she cut him off, exhaling. "I have just been hearing it for a very long time."

"But your grandmother only died yesterday?" Gabriel said, confused. He was also getting quite distracted by the trailing ribbon from her hair, dangling tantalisingly over her left breast. The knot in the depths of his stomach tightened harder and his thighs began to feel hot.

"Yes, she did," Scarlett nodded, sadness crossing her face. "But I have always been pitied for what happened with her and the wolf. The people of Boque... do not seem to want to forget it."

"Oh... I am sorry. I did not know. I mean... I *know* what happened... obviously. I mean, my father told me what happened. I did not realise it has remained a topic of conversation after so long."

"How I wish it were not," Scarlett said, staring into the air in front of her. "What I would not give to go one day in the village without hearing about it in some way or another." She sighed and let her head drop back, the sunlight striking her face, causing it to glow.

"Talking to you is rather refreshing. I think you may be the first person I have ever spoken to who has not mentioned it." She turned and smiled gratefully at him and immediately he felt his face grow hot and the all too familiar thickening from between his legs. He shifted his plate slightly, desperate for her not to notice.

Thankfully, a distraction arrived in the form of a snuffling sound coming from the other side of the barn wall. Gabriel jerked forwards, but Scarlett caught his arm. "It is alright, it is only Blaze," she stood up, pulling Gabriel to his feet with her. He rapidly repositioned his plate. "Come with me."

He followed her slowly into the barn. At the far end was a set of stables. Inside one was a large chestnut brown Clydesdale horse, who snuffled happily at Scarlett's presence as she petted his nose. "Blaze, this is Gabriel. Gabriel; Blaze."

"It is nice to meet you Blaze," Gabriel answered in almost a whisper as he gazed up in awe at the creature, who stood at least another foot taller than him.

"Let us get you some fresh hay," Scarlett said to him with a final pat, before heading to the ladder opposite the stalls that led up into the hay loft. She paused on the second rung. "Are you coming?" she asked teasingly.

Gabriel started, shaking himself slightly. "Oh! Yes, of course." He followed her up the ladder, keeping his eyes firmly on the rungs in front of him. When he reached the top, he found Scarlett pulling apart a hay bundle and throwing it chunk by chunk into Blaze's stable below. He crossed to her side, lifting the entire bale and dropping it to the waiting horse, who whinnied happily and started eating.

"Wow, hay is incredibly heavy," Scarlett gasped, puffing from her efforts. "Woodcutting really does make you strong, doesn't it?"

"Not specifically," Gabriel said, looking down at his upper arms. "What I mean is, not always, but it does train specific muscles. I can be strong in certain situations."

"Whatever is the difference?" Scarlett laughed, moving forward and holding his arm in her hands, gazing at it analytically.

Gabriel's breath caught in his throat at her touch, and he immediately felt the blood begin to rush downwards again. He spun on his heels, hoping she would not notice.

"Uhh… well," he scratched the back of his head, trying to collect his thoughts. "Think of it like this; I can *lift* heavy things, but I cannot wield a sword. It requires different muscle groups that I do not use in my work, so if I were to go up against anyone with a sword, I would barely be able to swing it let alone beat someone."

When he turned back to her, she was looking at him curiously, hopefully unaware of the battle between Gabriel's mind and body. She sat on another hay bale and patted the space next to her. "I will not bite, you know," she told him gently, a smile on her face.

He bit his lip, his eyes moving from the space beside her, to her face, before sliding into the spot on the hay next to her. "It is a lot warmer up here," Gabriel said, desperate to fill the silence lest it become tense and awkward.

"It is," Scarlett agreed, nodding. She pulled at the thread on her cloak and let it drop to the floor. "There were times when I was a child that I would sleep up here in winter because it would be warmer than the house. That was, of course, before Mother started hunting and we had the money to make changes to the farmhouse and keep the fires going day and night."

Gabriel gazed at her as she spoke. He could not help it. Her bare shoulders led into toned arms that ended in delicate, yet worn fingers. He could tell that however she spent her time on the farm, she worked as hard as he.

Before Gabriel realised Scarlett had noticed him staring, his eyes met hers again, locking for what seemed like an eternity. A strand of her hair hung down her face just beside her left eye. He moved to gently tuck it behind her ear. Scarlett inhaled sharply at his touch, her eyes closing for an instant before they fluttered open again.

Gabriel's hand dropped, grazing her cheek, before it came to rest on her chin. Scarlett drew closer, tilting her face towards his. Her lips parted slightly as she exhaled in anticipation.

"SCARLETT!" Ingrid's voice called out across the yard. "ARE YOU IN THERE?"

"Mother!" Scarlett gasped, leaping up, grabbing her cloak and heading for the ladder. "I am sorry! I have to-"

"It's alright," Gabriel said, waving his arms. "I understand. Go!" She gave him a quick smile, before she disappeared down the ladder. It took some time before Gabriel was willing to risk heading back into an event full of townspeople. It was quite a while before he was even able to stand up.

Gabriel Bloom's very existence was altered that day. In meeting Scarlett Black, his world grew exponentially, which was mirrored in his drive, ambition, and goals. There was going to be more to life than the job… and he had just met her.

4-SCARLETT

Scarlett had said goodbye to her grandmother's grave and made for home, the memories of the funeral and her almost kiss with Gabriel fresh in her mind. It was almost lunch time and her mother tended to get irritable if she was not home in time for them to start their afternoon training session directly after. Ingrid Black was a stickler for punctuality. She believed it was one of the highest values customers prized and considered it to be tantamount to integrity. Despite having lost her own mother less than a month before, this had not assuaged her tenacity. Every day, after lunch, was training time; sunny, raining or in a blizzard, Ingrid insisted Scarlett be ready for anything at *any* time.

Scarlett rushed up the stairs and flew through the front door just as Mason, the cook, was setting bowls of soup and plates of bread onto the table. "Scarlett! I do hope you have got the fresh loaves with you there. I have just used the last of what we had in the cool store."

Scarlett lifted her basket. "Right here Mason," she huffed, out of breath. "Do not fear." She handed it over to him before turning to hang her brown cloak on one of the kitchen hooks.

The moment she took her seat her mother came in through the back door, dropping her muddy boots into the basket. "You are cutting it rather close today!" she announced, pulling off her own cloak and hanging it by Scarlett's. Ingrid was slightly taller than Scarlett, with sandy blonde hair pulled back into a tight braid. She was always wearing riding gear, clothes that were easy to move around in. No one would ever catch her in a dress; too impractical.

"I am in my seat before you, Mother," Scarlett pointed out, smiling widely. "Therefore, I am not late." Ingrid raised an eyebrow, before taking a seat opposite her. "Mother, I have been meaning to ask you something," she went on, prompted by her morning reminiscing.

"Oh?" Ingrid dipped a piece of bread into the thick, creamy soup and began to chew. "Oh Mason, this is amazing; just what I need after a long, muddy ride. You are a genius."

"Thank you, Madam!" he replied cheerily.

"Yes, it really is very good," Scarlett agreed quickly, before turning the conversation back. "But Mother, I was thinking about Hector-"

"-Hector?" Ingrid snorted derisively. "Whatever for?"

"Well..." Scarlett began, put off by her Mother's clear contempt. "He was coming to the farm almost every day after he saved Grandmother and I. Then, all of a sudden... he stopped. Why is that?"

Ingrid suddenly became very quiet. It was not just that she stopped talking, because Ingrid Black was not the type for small talk to begin with. She was all business, all the time. Here, she wavered; softened almost, like her toughened visage had been damaged. "Well... you are considered an adult now," she said softly. "And I did always tell myself that if you were to ask me questions I knew the answers to that I would answer them honestly..." She closed her eyes and took a deep breath in, opening them when she exhaled.

"Hector had been pursuing me for months," she began. "When I made it clear that nothing would come of it, he was dismal about it, but he seemed to accept my decision.

"A few days passed. I was in the lodge, collecting equipment for a hunt, when another hunter I had worked with previously joined me. He had overheard Hector in the tavern... mocking your father, saying that if Spiro had been a better hunter, he would still be alive. It was only then that I realised... it was *Hector's* patrol crew your father was with when he died.

"Hector stopped coming back here after I told him I knew it was his company that was responsible for my husband's death and that I could not stand to see him a minute longer. I told him never to come back."

Scarlett remained in thought for a long while, shaken by the revelation. "But he did… for Grandmother's funeral rites," she finally said.

"Yes, he did," Ingrid said softly. "It was kind of him to do so after the way I treated him, but you have to understand the anger I was feeling at the time. I was building myself up to become both of the people your father and I *together* were supposed to be for you, so I could teach you to be both of those people for *yourself* one day. To learn Spiro was being mocked by the very person responsible for his safety; to learn that the man coming to my home, spending time around *my daughter* could be so cruel and heartless over being dismissed? I could not control my reaction to what I had learned."

"I understand, Mother." To hear that Hector had said such things about her father hurt Scarlett deeply, but it was not all there was to consider. "Hector still saved Grandmother and me. Surely that warrants some consideration?"

"Yes," Ingrid nodded. "And that is what I remembered the most when he came to the funeral rites. My mother only lived to have a proper burial with the funeral rites she deserved because he saved her." She gave Scarlett a small smile. "And I owe every day I spend with you to him."

"But you never took him up on his dinner offer," Scarlett pressed. "Why not?"

Ingrid scoffed, shaking her head. "Pride?" she finally responded.

"So if he were to offer to have us for dinner, you would consider it?"

"I do not know, Scarlett," she snapped irritably. "Why? Why this sudden curiosity?"

"He… he saved my life," she repeated, lifting her spoon to her mouth. Ingrid smiled sadly in response, a thoughtful look on her face.

♠

"WATCH YOUR SIDE!" Ingrid bellowed, lunging forward with her sword. Scarlett dodged the blow and swung around before matching her mother's thrust. "VERY GOOD! AGAIN!"

Scarlett and her mother had sparred every day from the time she was thirteen, with actual swords from the time she was fifteen. Ingrid's work had allowed them to amass a wide range of weapons of the highest calibre from the various smiths throughout Boque and the neighbouring towns.

"AND AGAIN!" Ingrid cried out, spinning to the left and catching her on the hip just before Scarlett was able to locks hilts and drive her mother to the ground. Holding her side, Scarlett sheathed her sword and hobbled over to her mother, offering a hand.

"Are you alright?" Scarlett huffed.

"I am only dirty; *you* are the one that got hit!"

"Yes," Scarlett laughed, nodding as she tried to catch her breath. "But I still beat you. Sometimes you have to let them get close if you want to disable them properly."

Ingrid grunted in reply. "Good, you have been listening."

Next, they ran the horses through the woods. Every other day they would run a different track, aimed at testing their reaction times. The woods were ever changing, so after a week any one of the track's landmarks would have changed, which would lead the unwary traveller into a multitude of dangers if they did not take absolute care. Hanging vines, a batch of poison ivy, a newly created sink hole from the rain and it could mean your doom. Ingrid had Scarlett prepare for it all.

When Blaze finally burst through the trees and back into the clearing that ran along the farm, Ingrid and her sleek black mare, Storm, were hot on their tails. By the time they reached the gates, they were neck and neck, but it was Ingrid and Storm that made it to the barn first, by a nose. "Good girl!" Ingrid cheered, patting Storm affectionately, before she climbed down and turned to Scarlett. "Not quite at his best today, is he?"

"Blaze *is* quite a decent amount heavier than Storm, Mother. One would *expect* her to be faster?"

"Yes, well we make a point in this family of shooting down standard expectations, do we not?" Ingrid retorted, hugging her daughter tightly. Scarlett breathed her in; the horsey scent that seemed to follow her everywhere even when she had not ridden Storm that day, and the smell of smoke and ash; the fire of the forges and the cigars of the men in the tavern.

Even now Ingrid would come across people who would try to devalue or short change her for her work, believing a woman either could not or should not be doing it. Instead of arguing, which her mother found to be beneath her, Ingrid would simply find her customers drunk at the tavern and take what was owed, by force, if necessary. The one time an inebriated customer fought her on it, the other citizens in the tavern put an end to his tirade rather quickly. One wrong move towards Boque's considered *saviour* was a sure fire way to find yourself exiled.

"I have thought about what we discussed at lunch," Ingrid said as they began to rub down the horses.

"Oh?"

"Yes," Ingrid nodded. "I think it… it might be time to move forward. After losing Mother… I feel I should show more gratitude to Hector for the years I was able to have with her, and all the years I will now have with you." Ingrid held Scarlett's cheek for a moment before she let her hand fall away and went back to seeing to Storm.

Scarlett's heart did an excited dance in her ribcage, a warm sensation rushing through her body.

5-GABRIEL

Gabriel and Hector were returning from a business trip. Despite the cool breeze, the exertion had left them hot and irritable. It was meant to be a normal delivery, but it seemed multiple things went wrong at every step; the wood was not the right type, then it was not cut thick enough, then the price was argued over. Gabriel did not look forward to going back and was grateful when his father had ended the contract on the spot.

"It is a matter of integrity, Son," he had told him. "If a man does not abide by his principles, then he hasn't any."

As Gabriel wiped away the perspiration building up on his brow, he was grateful his father had purchased horses for the deliveries farther from home. It certainly did not help him now, as his father also insisted that the horses should journey home unburdened after such a heavy haul. Hector and Gabriel pushed on alongside Birch and Ash, simply happy that the horrendous contract was over and that they did not have to lug the wagon all the way home themselves.

This had been their third trip since Rosa Black's funeral rites and Gabriel had spent almost every moment of them thinking about Scarlett... and the barn. What would have happened if her mother had not come looking for her? Would she really have kissed him? Was she thinking about him as much as he thought about her? The same *way* he thought about her?

His entire life had been so encapsulated by the family woodcutting business that Gabriel had never really thought of the world outside it, let alone yearned for it. For the first time there was something in his mind more than what his next axe would look like, or what order needed to be filled next.

Did Scarlett feel the same? She had said that every time she went into the village people would not let go of her past, making her feel eternally trapped in it. Is it then possible that he offered her some sort of reprieve; a fresh taste of life like she had given him? He certainly hoped so. She seemed desperate to be rid of her past, which was impossible to do when the people of Boque were consistently reminding her of the memories.

The men topped the final crest of the mountains and there, nestled in the valley below, was Boque; the larger town surrounded by a large circle of crumbling stone walls;

the outer village and farmland spreading outward from the town towards the forest. They were almost home.

Gabriel sighed as he saw the smoke coming from the far off chimney set on the outskirts of the town just below them. Not only did living off the edge of the forest mean easy access to their most valuable staple; trees, but not being in the town proper gave a certain sense of peace and privacy that Gabriel appreciated.

Together, he and Hector ran down the slope as fast as they could with Birch and Ash following with the wagon. "Soon now, Lad!" Hector huffed cheerily. "Grace has something cooking, I bet!"

"I am more interested in a hot bath, Father," Gabriel replied, wiping his forehead on the back of his hand again. "These trips leave me dirtier than cleaning the stable."

"*You?* Clean the *stables?*" Hector roared with laughter. "If I ever see the day, Son, I shall draw your bath myself!" He continued to chuckle to himself as they made their way through the gates and towards the homestead, a broad, two storey, stone building with multiple chimneys coming out of the roof. To the right was a stack of hay that must have been delivered while they were away. The wagon was placed at the blank space to the left and the horses were led into the stables.

Once inside, the men found that Grace had indeed been cooking. A full roast goose was turning on a spit in the fireplace, and the smell of freshly baked bread was wafting from the table.

Aunt Grace was just placing a bowl of potatoes and a stick of butter on the table when they walked through the door. "Welcome back! You are right on time. Tuck in!" Nothing tasted like Aunt Grace's cooking after a two day journey, but Gabriel found he could not focus on the delicious smells and mouth watering flavours.

As Hector animatedly informed his sister of the mess they had come from, Gabriel found his mind wandering yet again, to Scarlett. "I think I am finished," he finally sighed. "Would you mind if I excused myself Aunt Grace?"

"You've only had one plate!" she exclaimed. "Surely that is not enough!"

"Yes," Gabriel nodded, before jumping up from his chair, grabbing a roll from the bread basket, and kissing her playfully on top of the head. "But my smell will likely turn you from your meal also if something is not done about it." Aunt Grace laughed and playfully pushed him away. Gabriel wandered down the hallway, leaving her and his father to their gossip.

Once in the bathroom, a large room with a cobblestone floor, giant claw foot bathtub and a long wide fireplace, he stripped bare and dumped his dirty clothes in a pile by the door along with his boots. He shivered slightly in the cold, rubbing his arms as he crossed to the bath. He tested the water with a hand. It was perfect. The coals were always kept hot to ensure a good supply of warm water on the days they returned from deliveries. It was one of the many ways Aunt Grace took care of them.

It was something Gabriel was most grateful for, because it was one of his favourite places to think, and his mind was heavier than usual. It had been ever since the day of Rosa Black's funeral rites.

Gabriel slid into the water, groaning with pleasure at its warmth, and from the moment his body relaxed in the heat, his mind began to wander again, to Scarlett. The strand of hair hanging down her face, the shape of her neck as she pulled her hair over the opposite shoulder, the curve of her lip as she tilted her head up to kiss him; he imagined what would have happened if they had not been interrupted; if he had been able to kiss her.

The image came to him immediately, like a loyal hound, desperate for his attention. Their lips finally connecting, the warmth of her skin, the feeling of his hands cupping her face as they kissed passionately; and he felt himself begin to engorge, blood rushing downward so quickly he felt dizzy.

In his mind, he was kissing Scarlett; she kissing him back just as fiercely. He was lifting her up, straddling her across his hips as he carried her over to the soft hay in the top of the loft. In reality, his hands drifted down. He was thick; hard. He took a firm, gentle grip and began to work his member back and forth in time to his racing thoughts.

Scarlett was lying in the hay, straw in her hair. He was rapidly undoing the bodice of her shirt as she did the same with the cord of his pants. He watched her undershirt fall in his mind's eye, revealing soft, round breasts. His hands moved faster as his body throbbed. His breath began to come faster.

The Gabriel in his imagination was running his hands down Scarlett's body, following it with teasing by his lips and tongue. Scarlett's breathing was heavy, her breasts rising and falling rapidly. He pulled the cord on her riding pants and slid them down. The image was so clear. It felt real; so real, that a pulsing began in the head of his shaft as his hands moved more and more vigorously.

Gabriel was leaning into Scarlett; they were chest to chest now; Gabriel pressing his weight against her. Scarlett moaned deeply as he felt her envelop him fully, and Gabriel was pulled back to his body, lifting his organ out of the water as to not soil the bath as it pulsed in his hands.

When the rush had abated, and the blood had finally begun to return to the rest of his body, Gabriel leaned out of the bath to wipe his hands on his already dirty pants. He exhaled slowly as he settled back into the water to cleanse himself properly.

Just as he was rinsing the soap from his ears and hair, there was a tap on the door. "Gabriel?" It was Aunt Grace. "We have a visitor. Make yourself presentable, Boy!"

"Well, what do you *think* I am doing in here?" he called back, his face red, desperately thankful that she had not knocked a few minutes before.

"Just hurry up, will you? She will be here any minute!" He heard Aunt Grace's boots stomping off down the hallway.

She? Gabriel leapt from the tub and grabbed one of the fleecy towels from the rack by the fireplace, quickly covering himself before dashing to his room to dress. Who could be arriving to cause such a fuss? Aunt Grace was never snippy, except in jest.

He rapidly dressed into his business attire. Other than his formal wear, which had only been worn once before at his Uncle's funeral rites and likely did not fit him anymore, it was the nicest outfit he owned; soft leather pants with shiny black riding boots and a black cotton shirt.

It was what he wore when he travelled with Ash to the neighbouring villages and towns to barter for contracts. He was looked upon more favourably if he dressed professionally, but still needed to look competent and capable of the work. These clothes worked like a charm. He was able to get three new contracts on the first day he ever wore them. They had become something of a good luck charm.

The moment his feet were in his boots, he took off down the hallway to meet his aunt, who was, at that very moment, opening the door for their guests. "Welcome!" Hector boomed happily... as Ingrid and Scarlett Black stepped through the door.

6-SCARLETT

Scarlett had insisted her mother accompany her to Hector's cottage. "Come on Mother, the horses never get just a simple walk with us; it is always training, and surely if you wish to make amends with Hector and move forward then you have to actually *be there*."

Ingrid had fussed and argued, but in the end, she had saddled up Storm as Scarlett did Blaze, and they had spent the afternoon riding from one side of Boque to the other. It was a wonderfully welcome change. Her mother was well respected, but people could find her rather intimidating as there were few unaware of her skill. Also, being on horses made Scarlett less accessible to the people.

Both of these things meant she was able to cross the entire town without the onslaught of pitying looks and monotonous apologies that usually followed her. They had become worse since her Grandmother's death. Not only did it bring the incidents of the wolf plague back into the forefront of the town's mind, but it gave them a whole new tragedy to focus on as well.

When they entered the homestead, Hector welcomed them warmly and Grace took their cloaks. "How are you, Ladies?" he said, kissing each on them on the cheek. "You are as radiant as ever!" he told Ingrid specifically.

"We are well, Hector, thank you," Ingrid responded with a small smile. "Shall we sit? We've brought cakes."

"How wonderful!" Grace chimed in. The kettle began to whistle. "And perfect timing!" As Grace fixed the tea and bustled over with the teapot and cups, Hector, Gabriel, Ingrid and Scarlett all took seats around the fire. Ingrid opened the basket and handed out the warm, sweet treats and they made simple small talk as they ate and drank their fill.

When they had finished, Hector cleared his throat. "It is wonderful to see you again," he began. "But tell me, what brings you to visit us here?"

"Ah, yes," Ingrid nodded, glancing at Scarlett. She nudged her head forward encouragingly. "Well, many years have passed since our falling out and with... Mother's death, I feel it is time to let bygones be bygones."

"Oh," Hector responded quietly, his face dropping. "I see. That is a very kind and decent thing to do, Ingrid. I will never be able to apologise enough for my misdeeds, but *this-* this is wonderful!" Joy took over his entire face.

"Incredibly big of you!" Grace piped up, gazing at Ingrid with adoring respect. "After what this lummox pulled, I am surprised you did not throw the lot of us out on our backsides at your dear mother's ritual supper."

"It was... hard to see you again, Hector," Ingrid continued. "But it was also kind and *decent* of you to come after what had happened between us, and I will never be able to thank you enough for what you did for Scarlett... and Mother."

Grace seemed to tear up. "Oh, that is *lovely!*" She then turned to Scarlett and Gabriel. "Why don't you two go and see to the horses? Looks like we will settling in for a bit; you will want to get them out of the cold!"

"Yes, Aunt Grace," Gabriel answered immediately, getting to his feet.

Scarlett quickly stood up and followed him outside. "I cannot believe that I managed to get her here!" she whispered excitedly. "I can barely get her to leave the house for anything other than work and training!"

"You wanted her to come here?" Gabriel questioned as they walked to the stable.

Scarlett paused. Had she given herself away? She would have to tread more carefully. "I... encouraged her to take Hector up on his offer for dinner," she said carefully. "He has done so much for us and it seemed such a waste to dismiss an entire friendship over an argument that happened so long ago."

Gabriel nodded. "I see. You would hope my father and Ingrid could repair the relationship?"

"Yes!" Scarlett answered quickly. "He saved my life! And Mother said so herself that she owed all the years she was able to have with Grandmother to Hector saving us from the wolf."

They crossed the yard in peaceful silence with Blaze and Storm. Birch and Ash snuffled happily at their new friends as Gabriel and Scarlett loosened their saddles and tack for comfort and placed a bucket of oats into each feed bag.

Gabriel was the first to break the silence as they made their way back out of the stables. "How was your ride over?"

"Amazing!" Scarlett exclaimed in reply. "We were not stopped *once*. It was wonderful." She remembered exactly why they would be stopping her and her face suddenly changed. It was pensive, concentrating as she replayed her most recent dream in her mind.

"Is everything alright?"

Scarlett blushed. "Oh, yes! I... I have simply been having some dreams lately," she admitted. "About the wolf."

"Nightmares?" Gabriel questioned. "So the moment Boque allows you to forget, your mind will not?"

"And vice versa! They used to be nightmares... I suppose they still are," Scarlett considered, her head tilting to the side slightly in thought. "It used to be exactly the same one. I would be chased by the wolf. I would wake before it caught me."

"And what happens now?" Gabriel asked, curious.

"He... he catches me," Scarlett paused. "Then I wake up."

"Does it hurt?" They started up the stairs towards the door of the homestead.

Scarlett considered the question carefully, running back over her latest escapades with the wolf; the feel of the thick red fur turning to hardened muscle beneath her fingers. "Sometimes," she finally answered, smiling.

♠

Days passed, and market day came. Scarlett was in the Boque marketplace, surrounded by the produce of Black Farm.

"Six carrots please, dear!"

"Here you are Lady Trenton."

"Do you have any basil left?"

"I am sorry, Mistress Quinn bought the very last batch we had. I will have more next week."

"When were these eggs laid?"

"The oldest are four days old, Mr Hardwick."

Scarlett, Mason and one of the housemaids, Lina, were all at their market stall, ensuring the people of Boque had access to the produce their families needed. It was rather hectic every week, with their goods selling out within a few hours. Luckily, there were other vegetable farms in Boque so nobody ever went without what they needed to put food on the table.

"Good morning Scarlett!" a voice called out.

"Good morning Keenen," Scarlett sighed.

"Yes, hello Scarlett!"

"How *are* you, Scarlett?"

"Having a good time, *Scarlett?*"

Keenen was surrounded by the local nobility, if one would call it that. They were the children of the wealthiest and most highly respected families in Boque. Yarraan, Janarri and Victor were a mirror of Keenen in attitude. They all carried themselves as though they ruled Boque, like no one could stand against them. Girls fawned over them, and they took as many as would have them. Their parents behaved as though their precious boys could do no wrong and as such, they ran wild throughout the town, doing whatever… and whoever they pleased.

"Do come and join us, won't you Scarlett?" Victor said. "Surely the servants can handle whatever is left to sell?"

"They are not servants, Victor," Scarlett said briskly, raising an eyebrow and crossing her arms. "And my farm is my responsibility, including this stall. It is something I take very seriously."

"Of *course* you do!" Janarri jumped in emphatically. "Your little business definitely keeps you busy while your mother is away. Luckily, it won't be necessary for much longer!" He nudged Keenen in the ribs.

"Need I remind you Janarri, that my *little business* is considerably more lucrative than the *nothing* you do every day," Scarlett shot back smoothly. "At least I am providing something of value to Boque."

"Well Scarlett, make the right choices and you could spend your days like I do," he said. "A woman of leisure; without the worry of finances just think of what you could be doing with all that time." He smiled knowingly at Keenen.

"Thank you Janarri, but I believe I already make the right choices, and I have far more practical things to be doing than chasing skirts around Boque," Scarlett turned away from the group. "Have a nice day gentlemen."

She heard them walk away, muttering under their breath, until a voice said questioningly, "Scarlett?" She turned to find Keenen, still in place. "You know I am not like them, that I do not think the way they do?"

"Are you not?" Scarlett asked. "Your behaviour says otherwise."

"Come *on* Scarlett! You know I do not want you stuck in a house cooking and cleaning all day! I know what the farm means to you," he pressed.

"Then why spend your time with them Keenen?" Scarlett asked him, placing her hands on the stall in front of her and leaning towards him. "We have known each other since we were children. You are not like them," she turned away again. "At least, you weren't."

Scarlett went about pulling together the final batches of stock and bringing it to the front of the stall, when yet another familiar voice rang out. "Well now, what was *that* all about?"

"Grace!" Scarlett declared happily, finding her walking over from the craftsmen. "Oh, you know how they can be. They cannot take no for an answer."

"Why would you?" Grace asked, laughing. "Take the life of luxury while it is offered, Girl!"

Scarlett laughed too. "I do not think my mother would accept such a way of thinking. Her expectation of my independence is quite high, Grace."

Grace changed her tack immediately. "Oh, of *course!*" she nodded. "Well, your mother is a highly capable woman; brave and smart. She will not lead you astray, that is for sure, my Dear!"

"Aunt Grace, there you are!"

Gabriel.

Scarlett stopped, staring at him. He was just as handsome now as when she had last seen him. "Hello Gabriel," she said.

"Scarlett!" he exclaimed. He seemed flustered. "I-I did not expect to see you here?"

"I am here every market day," she told him. "This is the first time I have ever seen you here Gabriel."

"Yes," he nodded, picking up a head of lettuce. "If I am home from business travel, then usually I am resting for the next trip or doing home repairs while Father works. I rarely get to experience the joy of sharing a morning on the town with my aunt." He smiled at Grace.

"Oh, you sweet talker," she chuckled, carefully selecting some strawberries.

"But… now that I know you are here every week," Gabriel continued quietly. "I will be sure to attend more often." Scarlett smiled shyly.

"Take these, will you Gabriel?" Grace said, handing him the strawberries and some coins. "I am going to the tavern to collect your father. Stay out of trouble!"

"Of course, Aunt Grace," he nodded, kissing her on the cheek.

"Give your mother my love, Dear!" Grace called as she headed towards the centre of town.

"I will!" Scarlett waved back. When Grace had disappeared into the crowd, she turned back to Gabriel. "Whatever will you do with all your free time?" she asked, as Mason and Lina started to pack down the back of the stall into the wagon.

"I would very much like to explore the town. It has grown since the last time I was here for a festival and even then, it was dark," Gabriel mused, looking around him. "Would you like to join me for a walk?"

Scarlett looked to Mason and Lani. "I-uh… I have work that needs doing here. I cannot leav-"

"-Nonsense!" Lina cut in, standing up, empty crates in her hands. "Mason and I can see to the packing."

"Are you sure?" Scarlett asked, excitement building within her.

"Yes, of course!" Mason boomed. "Go!"

Scarlett joined Gabriel on the other side of the stall, and together, they made their way through the marketplace and into the town square. "How are the dinner preparations coming?" Scarlett asked politely, breaking the silence.

"Very good!" Gabriel answered. "Aunt Grace has been planning ever since you joined us at home. "The dinner is almost a week away and she already has four courses planned!" he laughed. "The roast alone will take all day. She is very excited."

"Are you… excited?" Scarlett asked tentatively.

"For dinner?" Gabriel answered. "Food is food," he shrugged. Scarlett's heart sank. "But I am definitely looking forward to spending the evening with you." Scarlett grinned, looking at her feet so he could not see her blush.

They made their way through the town, Scarlett showing Gabriel the street repairs and new torch lights that had been built throughout the square; new buildings had been constructed and shops had expanded. Gabriel listened keenly with interest, hanging onto Scarlett's every word.

"The mill was not here before? They did not *move* it, did they?" Gabriel asked, shocked as he stared at the mill, grain silo and adjacent storehouses.

Scarlett chuckled. "No," she said. "They had to build a larger one to accommodate the town's growth. Since

Mother cleared the wolves from the forest, many people started coming to Boque to settle and so its needs grew," she explained. "The other mill is to the south; this one was built last year."

"Ah yes, I do remember the construction noise now I think on it," he said. They began to make their way to the tavern, where they would find Gabriel's father Hector and his Aunt Grace. "Are... are you looking forward to dinner?" Gabriel asked as they meandered peacefully through Boque, stopping by the western well.

"Definitely so!" Scarlett said, leaning against the well. "Especially now that you have described what Grace has planned for it!" she teased.

Gabriel dropped the bucket back to the bottom of the well, the chain unravelling rapidly before the deep *splash* echoed from within the chamber. He moved in front of her, reaching out to grasp her hand. "Is the food all that attracts you?" he asked softly.

Scarlett held her breath as Gabriel lifted her hand to his lips and kissed it gently. "No." Her voice was barely a whisper. He moved closer, drawing his other arm around her waist. Their lips were an inch apart.

"WELL, WELL, WELL," a mocking voice rang out. "What do we have here?"

It was Keenen's friend Yarraan. Keenen, Victor and Janarri were with him. "Now Gabriel, you would not be making unwise choices, would you, Friend?" he asked threateningly, coming closer.

Scarlett was getting irritated with how pushy Keenen and his friends were becoming. He was not always like this. Before Yarraan, Victor and Janarri had moved to Boque with their parents, rich and privileged enough to seek a home in the safest town in the country, Keenen was a kind and simple boy. The life they led had changed him in all the worst ways.

Before Scarlett could step in, Gabriel disengaged from her and turned to face them. "I do not believe any of my choices are your business, Yarraan."

"I would agree with you, but tampering with a match becomes everyone's business, does it not?" he continued. "Keenen; do you have anything you would like to say?" he asked, placing heavy emphasis on the question.

Keenen looked at him, looking uncomfortable and pressured. Then he shook his head. "No, not a thing," he said, before striding towards Gabriel, his fists clenched.

Scarlett got to her feet. Gabriel stood his ground, Keenen gaining on him as his gang of delinquent, hedonistic layabouts whooped and cheered. He had come within striking distance when a sharp yell came from their left. "BOYS! How are you Lads? Having a good time this fine market day?" Hector came into view, pulling the bucket out of the well with one hefty yank.

"H-hello Hector," Scarlett said, eyeing off the other boys. Hector dumped his entire head in the bucket then shook himself off like a dog. "How… how was your tavern visit?"

"Scarlett!" he boomed. "I did not see you there! Same as always, my dashing girl, same as always!" he seemed in a very cheery mood. "Whatever are you doing here with this bunch of louts?"

"Uh…" Keenen and his friends glared at her. "Grace asked me to show Gabriel the new buildings since he has not been in town in a while. I had finished up at the stall so…"

"Kind of you, Scarlett; very kind of you!" he went on. "Well, we will have to have you gents over to the house for some cards one of these days, what say you Keenen?" Hector clapped him on the shoulder.

Keenen gave him a forced smile. "Very kind of you to offer, Hector. Come on boys," and he turned on his heels and strode off down the alley between the buildings, Yarraan, Victor and Janarri following.

"Shall we see you home?" Gabriel asked Scarlett.

Scarlett shook her head. "No. No, I should still be in time to catch Mason and Lina," she told them. "Have a lovely day." She headed back towards the marketplace, glancing back at Gabriel and Hector walking in the opposite direction. Gabriel looked back at her, confusion and sadness on his face.

7-SCARLETT

The night of the dinner at the woodcutter's home-stead arrived. Scarlett spent all afternoon preparing for it. She had hung her dress by the window so it could air out. She hadn't worn red since the infamous hooded cloak her grandmother had made for her, but she felt adventurous, and since her dreams with the wolf had taken their devilish turn, she was not as put off by the colour anymore. On the contrary… it excited her.

She found herself having to fan her face as it grew hot from the memories of the dreams that played in her head as she polished the matching shoes; the wolf turning into a man, him pulling her cloak away to reveal her bare nakedness, and the wolf changing again.

She forced her mind back to the shoes. They were a small heeled boot with a pointed toe, as was the fashion in the city at the time her mother had bought them. She had returned with them after a business trip to the city that took almost two weeks.

Scarlett shook her head in irritation, trying to keep her thoughts under control. The wolf's fur was receding back into his skin, leaving only that on his head, chest and groin, feeding her body his thickened shaft, inch by inch, no part of her taboo… Then it was Gabriel.

Scarlett abandoned the shoes entirely. They were quite beautiful, but before tonight there had never been a reason to wear such finery. She was not entirely sure tonight counted as such a reason, but she would wear them all the same.

She had then turned to her hair, which she had freshly washed, perfumed and air dried as she combed it out in the weak winter sunshine before pulling up the gentle curls with an ornate silver clip that held them out of her eyes. Next was her face, which she powdered, and her lips, which she tinted.

When she finally left her room, night had fallen and Mason had readied the carriage in preparation of escorting them. "You look beautiful, my dear," he told her lovingly.

"Thank you, Mason," Scarlett smiled graciously.

"You should see you mother!" he winked.

"Oh?" Curious, she climbed into the carriage, where she promptly gasped, dropping into her seat in surprise. "Mother?"

"Yes? Oh, don't you look lovely!" Ingrid had finally taken out her braid, leaving long thick waves cascading down the back of a deep royal blue dress. At her neck was a gold pendant given to her by Scarlett's father on their wedding day. Scarlett had spent her entire childhood admiring it, until the day he had died and her mother had taken on the workload of the farm, finding it too precious to risk wearing. It made her happy to see her mother wearing it again.

Mason called to the horses and they steadily made their way through Boque. Scarlett began to feel nervous. Would Gabriel find her outfit beautiful, or impractical? What if they had not planned on such a formal affair?

As the thoughts chased each other around her mind as the wolf did in her dreams, the carriage came to a stop. They had arrived. It was too late to turn back now. She could not change; she had no other clothes. She would simply have to enter the homestead and hope for the best.

She stumbled slightly down the carriage stairs, Mason at her elbow to help her. When she looked up, she gasped. Fires had been lit in every brazier along the stone ledge of the homestead's veranda, lighting up the entire property, showing several other carriages parked alongside Hector and Gabriel's. It was breathtaking. "Oh, how *gorgeous!*"

Ingrid exclaimed softly as she joined Scarlett at the foot of the stairs.

"Good evening ladies and gentlemen!" Hector's voice boomed as he stepped out of the doorway and came to the top of the stairs. "We are thrilled everyone could join us tonight!"

"Everyone?" All along the veranda of the homestead were groups of townsfolk. Scarlett recognised Jacques and Rohan, Mistress Quinn, a heavily pregnant Vera Hardwick with her husband Jonathon, and Lahar the tanner.

Mason offered Ingrid his arm and she took it gracefully. She seemed to have lost all the discomfort she had been expressing in the carriage. Together, they walked up the stairs, where Mason released her arm and bowed respectfully to Hector, who tilted his head in return.

Scarlett was still staring at the lights and all the people, when a voice came out of the shadows beside her, "May I escort you inside?" Scarlett gasped again, turning to the voice.

Gabriel.

He was wearing black formal pants with a deep forest green tunic over the top. From his tousled hair to his shiny boots, he looked incredibly handsome. "Why yes, thank you," she answered, taking the arm he was offering shyly.

"You… your dress," Gabriel began.

"You like it?" Scarlett asked coyly.

"Very much. You look very beautiful. Not that you do not *always* look beautiful… because you do. I mean-"

"-Thank you, Gabriel," Scarlett smiled at him. "You clean up rather nicely yourself." He blushed.

The guests, whom Scarlett found, to her dismay, also included Keenen, his friends, and their parents, were led onto the outer deck on the other side of the house. The hardwood floors had been polished, leaving them glinting in the light of the six foot wide fireplace that had been built into the wall with dark brown, stone slabs. A table large enough to seat every person in attendance took up most of the space on the other side of the deck.

Despite being outside in winter, they were quite warm, as a stone railing was built all along the edge of the deck and large window shutters reached from the railing all the way to the ceiling, blocking the view of the grounds below and sealing in the heat of the fires.

Dinner was a boring affair. It was delicious; the beef was perfectly cooked, the gravy was thick and spiced; Scarlett ate until she could not fit another morsel. It was evidently clear why Grace had planned and prepared for the entire week leading up to this night. Scarlett spent the time the adults spent discussing boring business and political affairs catching Gabriel's eye, smiling and looking away as she blushed.

Every now and then she would need to respond when a question was directed her way "What was that cake you made again, Scarlett?" or "That truly is an amazing dress, Scarlett". Each time she would respond appropriately, before returning to Gabriel, who would smile back shyly, then clearly try to force himself to pay attention to the conversation.

"I hear that a proposal is on the horizon!" Grace was saying, sitting to her mother's left.

"Excuse me?" Ingrid retorted bluntly. "Not on your *life!*"

"Oh no Dear, not you, *Scarlett!*"

Scarlett choked on a piece of potato, glancing quickly down the table to Keenen and his friends, who were seated with their parents. "*Where* would you hear such a thing?"

"I was in the bakery!" Grace continued animatedly. "As Rohan has it, he believes there is simply no one else for their beloved Keenan!" Scarlett felt sick. She looked Gabriel straight in the eyes. His face looked blank; inscrutable.

"Surely not!" Jensen, one of the dairy farmers, cut in. "Scarlett needs someone with sturdier stuff than that boy!"

He was fixated on his food, sawing away at the chunk of beef on his plate before reaching for a hot buttered roll from one of the many baskets placed around the table.

Ingrid laughed heartily. "Definitely not, Grace. In our family, we do *not* marry off our daughters."

"Oh no, of course," Grace babbled, clearly concerned she had caused offense. "I only meant-"

"-It is alright Grace," Ingrid clasped her hand over Grace's affectionately. "But let me assure you, if I had it my way there would be no marriage at all, let alone an *arranged* one. I want Scarlett standing on her own two feet from day one; that way no matter what happens in life, she is ready and can depend on herself." Scarlett sighed inwardly with relief, never having felt so grateful for her mother's stance on women's independence, but she could not bring herself to look at Gabriel again.

As the night wore on, and Hector and some of the other men became increasingly intoxicated from his emptying mead barrels, Grace and Ingrid sat by the fire with Mistress Quinn and Vera Hardwick, talking and drinking wine. Scarlett sat with them, quiet and polite, Gabriel standing with Hector, Keenen, and the wealthier men of Boque. He appeared to be avoiding her gaze. "Gabriel, be a dear and put the horses away for the night, will you?" Grace finally asked, calling to him. "It is getting late and the stable really should be locked up by now to keep the chill out."

"Of course, Aunt Grace," he answered, making for the back door that led into the homestead proper.

"I will come with you!" Scarlett found herself saying, getting to her feet.

"Scarlett?" Ingrid began. "It is *very* cold outside-"

"-Oh, leave the kids be, Ingrid," Grace huffed, waving her arm. "They clearly grow bored of our aging antics."

"Speak for yourself!" Ingrid laughed back, before telling Scarlett, "Take your cloak, please!"

Scarlett nodded eagerly and jumped up from the chair by the fire. She followed Gabriel across the house, to the hooks by the entry, collecting her cloak and joining Gabriel by the door. "After you," he bowed deeply.

"Why, thank you," she said, stepping out into chill of the late winter night.

"Are you sure you will be alright out here?" Gabriel asked, heading down the stairs without hesitation.

"Yes, I will be fine," she insisted, following him down the stairs and across the cold, wet grass. "Wait!" Gabriel paused to allow her to catch up. He looked hurt. "Gabriel, what is it?"

Gabriel breathed deeply and exhaled just as heavily. "Keenen?"

"What about him? You heard my mother. He has an interest that he will never see fulfilled, regardless of what Rohan and Jacques offer," Scarlett said.

"And you, Scarlett? What is it you want?" Gabriel continued across the grass and through the stable doors.

"Not him," she answered, lifting her skirts to stop them from getting wet. "He makes me uncomfortable... his eyes..."

"What?" Gabriel pressed, turning to look at her.

"They are... empty," she said softly. "Like the wolf's; hungry... predatory." Scarlett paused. "He just wants more prestige and he thinks I will deliver that for him. I will not. With everything he and his trashy friends do with the other girls of Boque, I am simply the road untraveled; a road that will *remain* untraveled," she finished forcefully.

Gabriel's jaw softened, and he let his shoulders relax and drop. "I am sorry."

"Not you too," Scarlett groaned jokingly. "No more apologies! No more pity!"

Gabriel laughed. "Stop it! I am being serious!"

"I am sick of being serious!" Scarlett exclaimed, her fists to her temples. "I have spent most of my life doing the right thing and behaving the right way. I never got a chance to be carefree or dismissive of the world. I was never..."

"You were never what?" Gabriel asked softly.

"Innocent," Scarlett whispered back, looking down at the still jagged scar on her right forearm and placing her left hand over it. "Not since the wolf."

"Are you still having the nightmares?" Gabriel asked, moving towards her. She nodded. "And he catches you every single night?"

"A different way each time," Scarlett told him, looking out the stable doors to the lightening bugs outside as they lit up the fields. "Last night he started as my grandmother… of all people. She was talking to me in her cottage. Then I noticed how large her eyes had become. I said to her 'Grandmother, what big eyes you have.'"

"What did she say?"

"She said 'the better to see you with, my Dear'. Then I noticed that her ears were big and pointy, so I said 'Grandmother, what big ears you have.'"

"And how did she respond?" Gabriel was closer to Scarlett now. She struggled to find the words to answer.

"She said 'the better to hear you with, my Dear.' Then she smiled, and her teeth were long and sharp, so I said 'Grandmother, what big teeth you have.'"

"And what did she say?" He was less than a foot away now.

"She said 'the better to eat you with, my Dear.'" Scarlett whispered, moving back into the wooden pillar holding up the stable ceiling. "Then it was not my grandmother anymore. The skin fell away and it was the wolf. He lunged at me… eating me piece by piece."

"What did you do?" Gabriel asked.

She did not respond immediately, daring to look up into his eyes. The fires of the stable lanterns danced in them. "I let him," she finally breathed.

Then Gabriel was against her; chest to chest; his lips against hers; Scarlett's body pressed between him and the pillar. His lips were soft and gentle. She could still taste the spice of the gravy on his lips. Scarlett felt his manhood pressed directly into the bottom of her stomach as it rapidly expanded, becoming harder. Gabriel pulled away.

"What's wrong?"

"I, uh-" Gabriel stuttered as he tried to turn away. Scarlett caught his arm.

"Shh," she whispered, drawing him back to her, one hand reaching up around his neck to pull his lips back to hers, the other reaching downward to grasp the still growing bulge beneath his tunic. He exhaled heavily, his hot breath turning to fog in the cold night air.

Gabriel pushed his body back up against hers, until it was difficult for Scarlett to breathe. He was grinding against her from thigh to stomach. She would have been concerned of the growing wetness within her undergarments soaking through her dress if she had been capable of thinking coherently, but all that crossed her mind was a primal, animalistic desire... when Gabriel dropped to a knee and lifted her skirts, placing her leg over his shoulder so he could devour her completely...

8-GABRIEL

It was quite some time before Gabriel and Scarlett were able to return to the homestead, and when they did, they found much of the party had dissipated. Mason was asleep by the door, his father and his remaining friends were still drinking on the rug by the fire. Ingrid and Aunt Grace were nowhere to be seen.

"Where are they?" Scarlett queried. "Could they be out looking for us?" she suddenly asked, worried.

"Well, we were exactly where Aunt Grace sent us. That would have been the first place they looked… I have a feeling we would know if they found us there," Gabriel said softly, his face forcedly serious. Scarlett giggled, nudging him with her shoulder.

They went back into the house, heading upstairs. "Aunt Grace?" Gabriel called.

"Mother?"

They heard muffled noises and banging coming from the room at the end of the corridor. Gabriel looked at

Scarlett questioningly. She shrugged her shoulders in reply. As Gabriel gripped the handle and turned, they heard a long loud moan come from the other side.

"Are we sure we want to do this?" Scarlett whispered.

"We have come this far," Gabriel answered, letting the door swing open and revealing a mass of limbs writhing about on the bed, the moans now twice as loud. They stood there, frozen, as the naked bodies of at least six of their neighbours created the most decadent scene Gabriel and Scarlett had ever witnessed.

When they regained control of themselves, Gabriel reached forward and closed the door. "Do you think they noticed us?" Scarlett asked.

"No… No, I do not think so."

"My mother was not in there."

"Nor my aunt."

They crept quietly down the hallway, stepping lightly on the stairs as they made their way back to the kitchen. "This is not the kind of dinner I expected when we were invited," Scarlett said, a stunned look still on her face.

"I-I am sorry, Scarlett," Gabriel said genuinely. "I had no idea. I would not have- I did not know that-"

"-That when you took me in the stable it was just one act your home would witness tonight?" she smirked playfully, wrapping her arms around him and planting a kiss on his cheek. "It is alright Gabriel. I believe that you did not know what your father had planned for this evening."

Gabriel exhaled with relief, wiping his clammy hands on his pants when Scarlett released him. They returned to the deck, where his father still sat with Jensen, Janarri's father Olvan and Mister Quinn, Mistress Quinn's brother. "Father, you haven't seen Aunt Grace, have you?"

"I cannot find my mother, either," Scarlett said.

"What?" his father snapped, whipping around to face them. "What did you say?"

"We cannot find Mother or Grace," Scarlett repeated.

"WHERE HAS THAT BLOODY WOMAN GOTTEN TO NOW!" he roared, getting to his feet and storming into the house. Gabriel was shocked at his rage. He had never seen his father behave this way. "GRACE! WHERE ARE YOU?" His father yelled up the stairs and out the front door, before finally coming back into the kitchen and screaming, "GRACE!"

"I am right here, Hector, whatever is the problem?" Grace snapped tartly, walking in from the hallway, fixing her hair.

"And where exactly have *you* been?" Hector demanded to know. He seemed unnecessarily angry.

"The bathroom if you *must* know," she replied just as dramatically.

"With Ingrid I presume?"

"Dresses are hard to shift, Hector! It can be helpful to have an extra pair of hands!" she said harshly, frowning.

Gabriel and Scarlett watched the interaction like one would a match of badminton; back and forth, over and over. "THAT IS SO DISRESPECTFULLY LIKE YOU GRACE!" Hector bellowed, six inches from her face. "IT IS NOT ENOUGH FOR YOU TO SWOON OVER EVERY CURVED HIP, BUT TO SEEK THE VERY ONE I CHOSE FOR MYSELF IS DESPICABLE!"

"HECTOR! Calm yourself!" she yelled back. "We have *guests!* You need to control yourself IMMEDIATELY!"

'I WILL DO NOTHING OF THE SORT!" Hector ranted, his face bright red. "I FINALLY HAVE THE CHANCE AFTER ALL THESE YEARS AND YOU ARE MOVING IN ON *MY* TERRITORY!" IT WAS WORK ENOUGH TO GET RID OF THE LAST ONE WHO DID SO!"

Scarlett froze.

"What did you just say?" a dangerously low voice asked. Grace stepped aside, revealing Ingrid standing in the entrance to the hallway. "Tell me, Hector, what does *'it was work enough to get rid of the last one'* mean, exactly?"

"I-I…I," Hector stammered.

Tears rose to Scarlett's eyes. Gabriel watched as she moved towards her mother, looking back at him and Hector. "You… you had my father killed?"

Gabriel, shocked, raised his hands. "No! No, of course not! Father would *never-!*"

"-He was in your patrol," Ingrid cut Gabriel off, still looking directly at Hector. "You were not simply negligent in your duty. He did not die because of his own lacking skills… He was ambushed, by people he trusted."

"No! I promise you-!" Gabriel begged, as Hector stood there, defeated, face downcast.

"-He had my father killed so he could pursue my mother," Scarlett said angrily. Gabriel fell silent, looking from Scarlett to his father, stuck with what to do.

"Come, Scarlett," Ingrid said softly. "MASON!" He appeared in a flash as she made for the door, opening it for her, and closing it behind them once they were through. Grace tried to chase them, still apologising, but Gabriel and his father could only stand there as they disappeared into the night.

9-GABRIEL

Weeks had passed since Gabriel had seen Scarlett. Twice he had seen her in town at the marketplace, but both times she had disappeared quickly the moment she had seen him. He was heartbroken. He knew in his heart that Scarlett was all he wanted in life; more than the business, more than the house... even more than his father's approval, but to disregard family loyalty was the highest of sins in Boque, and with Ingrid and Scarlett's accusations being considered unfounded in the eyes of the town, a son disowning his father could see him exiled. Then he would be even less likely to see Scarlett again.

Aunt Grace had changed. Her eyes were sunken, her clothes were hanging loosely on her thinning frame. What had happened with Ingrid and Scarlett had deeply upset her, but nothing did so more than his father's response. He solely blamed Aunt Grace for what had happened, as though his drunken confession or the fact that there was something to admit in the first place were not his responsibilities to bear. Gone were the jovial conversations, the witty banter, the loving brother sister relationship.

Like Gabriel, Aunt Grace was trapped; more so, even, than Gabriel was. As an adult he could begin to distance himself, but as an unmarried woman, Grace faced greater persecutions.

Gabriel pointed out that Ingrid had set herself apart and if she wanted to as well, then she could. "Ingrid Black is a remarkable woman… I am no Ingrid Black," Aunt Grace had answered. They seemed to be at an impasse; no way forward, no way back.

A chance came for change almost a month later, when the Hardwick baby was born. Little Genevieve had arrived late in the morning, perfectly healthy and long awaited by Vera and Jonathon. This was cause for celebration, as the wolf plague had decimated the town's population and so every baby was considered a miracle.

A festival was held in the square, and every citizen contributed something as a blessing to the child. For his family, Gabriel had carefully selected the sweetest smelling rosewood tree he could find and split it into perfectly sized logs; enough to keep the growing family warm for the rest of this winter and almost certainly all of the next.

He unloaded his gift into the Hardwick's wood pile before releasing Ash from the wagon and tying her to a communal hitching post by the tavern. His father was inside; exactly where Gabriel did not want to be, so he turned away and strode over to the fires, where his Aunt Grace was helping several other cooks with the large boars strung up on spits. "Is there anything I can do?"

"You can go and find Scarlett," she responded bluntly, not looking up from her vegetables. Gabriel gagged on his own tongue, but disguised it as a cough. "Well, get on with it! We need the herbs!"

"Oh!" Gabriel flushed, feeling foolish. "Of course, Aunt Grace. I will be back as soon as I can." He bowed slightly to the other cooks, then took his leave, ducking and weaving between the houses, looking for the tell-tale dark locks that were Scarlett's.

He found her coming out of the bakery. When she saw him, she froze, then determinedly set her eyes on a point in front of her and strode past him. "Scarlett, wait!"

"Leave me be, Gabriel. I am busy," she said.

"The-the cooks; they sent me for the herbs," Gabriel spat out.

Scarlett stopped short, looking down into her basket. "Oh." Her voice was small. She reached into the basket and withdrew a large bundle tied with thin twine. "Here. I was just making the delivery to the bakery so the bread would be ready in time."

"Yes," Gabriel nodded. "I see that. Thank you. Enjoy the festival." He turned and walked back towards the fires, his face burning.

"Gabriel!" He stopped, not turning back around. "I am not here for Keenen."

Gabriel closed his eyes for a moment before he could bring himself to respond. "That is really none of my business anymore, is it?"

♠

The baby was blessed by Boque's Priestess as the sun went down. The boars had become moist and succulent, the fat dripping from their bodies, causing the fires to spit and hiss. The rolls and apples sat piled high in baskets all around the square. Whole fire pits were dedicated to keeping tea kettles hot and trays of baked treats warm. Women of the town were passing around the baby girl, while men sat around the fires eating their fill and toasting again and again.

Gabriel passed his father by one of the fireplaces, sitting with a group of his friends. "Come sit with us Lad! Have a drink!" he called merrily.

"Yes Father, of course!" he called back, knowing it was unwise to appear less than companionable with his father.

"But I must pay my respects to the Hardwicks first!" It worked like a charm. Hector raised his tankard and nodded.

Tradition dictated that every citizen must acknowledge every newborn on their blessing day. Gabriel had specifically avoided it until his father requested an audience to ensure he had an ironclad excuse to deny him.

Gabriel approached Vera Hardwick, who had little Genevieve cradled in her arms. "Congratulations Mrs Hardwick. Blessings on your household," he said.

"Thank you, Gabriel," she said softly as the baby stirred. Gabriel peered into her arms. Genevieve was the smallest human Gabriel had ever seen. He had attended many other newborn blessings since the wolf plague ended, but the little baby girl before him was the smallest of them all.

As he watched, she stretched her arms up and out of her blanket, exposing her tiny fists. Gabriel touched a fingertip to it, causing the fist to open and clasp around his finger. He chuckled softly. "Strong grip you have there, Little One."

Vera regarded him curiously. "Would you like to hold her?" she asked. Gabriel was shocked. It was rare for any men outside of the immediate family to hold a baby. For women it was more common, but not men. Still, he nodded.

Vera placed the baby in Gabriel's arms. "She is so light!" he exclaimed softly.

Vera chuckled lightly. "Out here, yes. She did not feel so from the inside, let me assure you."

Gabriel reached down to stroke the baby's face when a voice cut through his reverie. "Of *course* you would be holding the baby! No need to worry about him now, Scarlett! I told you he was not man enough!"

Gabriel took a breath, before carefully handing Genevieve back to Vera. He then turned to see Scarlett, sitting by a fire with her mother and his Aunt Grace, and Keenen, who was laughing raucously along with Janarri, Yarraan and Victor. "Now is not the time," he said to them flatly. "You need to be more respectful to the Hardwicks. You should apologise!"

"Apologise?" Keenen laughed, walking towards him aggressively. "For what? Pointing out how ridiculous the idea is of you being considered over me? Those are *facts*, Gabriel," he yelled arrogantly. "That is all; nothing to apologise for."

Gabriel walked towards him at the same rapid pace. He was not about to let Keenen ruin Genevieve's day. He would drag him out of there like a doll if he had to. He could do it, too. It would only take the same muscles he used for his work.

He never got the chance. Scarlett got there first. "How *dare* you!" she hissed, malice dripping in her words as she kept her voice low enough to not cause a scene.

"This is a *blessing* day! One of our most sacred celebrations, and here you are making it about yourself! This! This, Keenen, is why I will *never* choose you! And you would do well to learn some humility, or you will find that no one else will either!"

Leaving Keenen to stew in his humiliation, Scarlett grabbed Gabriel's hand and dragged him away, not stopping until they had reached an alley between the tavern and the central grain store. "That should not have happened. It is not wise to anger Keenen. His fathers are too well respected. It is a battle you will not win."

"I am not looking for a battle," Gabriel said, crossing his arms. "But I will not let Keenen walk all over me or anyone else in this town just because of who his parents are."

Scarlett raised her hands and let them drop to her sides. "And where would that leave you?"

"I can make my own bread."

In spite of herself, Scarlett smiled. Then it suddenly dropped from her face, to be replaced by confusion. "Is that your father?"

Gabriel turned to where she was pointing. Walking down the lane that led away from the town square, was a tall, broad shouldered figure. "Let him go," he sighed, waving an arm. "Better at home, passed out, than causing trouble here." Gabriel turned back to Scarlett, softening. "How have you been... since the dinner?"

Scarlett gulped, all traces of the smile gone. "Coming to terms with what your father did to mine was not easy, but I would rather know than continue in ignorance any further."

"Further into what?" Scarlett stared at him knowingly. He held her gaze. "Scarlett, you have to know that I knew nothing about this. Now that I do, I am doing everything I can to extricate myself and my aunt from him, but Aunt Grace cannot just leave; she is too scared, and I cannot leave her there with him."

"Then what *are* you doing?" Scarlett asked bluntly.

"Looking for any proof to the claim," Gabriel answered. "Admission or not, my father would be believed over all five of the people who heard him. I have spent weeks going through contracts and work logs, matching them with the town's death records in an attempt to find a pattern; some sort of evidence that he was linked to your father's death... or anyone else's."

"Anyone else's?" Scarlett repeated. "What do you mean?"

"Father seemed highly defensive over Aunt Grace helping your mother with her dress. If he *killed* your father to get to her… it is possible he would have done it to others… for other reasons," Gabriel suggested quietly.

"What are you saying?"

"This was the peak of the wolf plague. The patrols were made up of a lot of woodcutters… many of whom died," Gabriel explained. "Who got all of the extra work when they did?" He looked pointedly at Scarlett, who was shifting her eyes, adding it all together. "Who had the most to gain from their deaths?"

Scarlett gulped. "What have you found?"

"All of the deaths I have investigated so far all occurred on nights my father was on a work trip or out on patrol after the wolf plague started, but the research is moving slowly; I still have all my lopping and splitting to do, plus my house chores… Aunt Grace is not coping with them by herself."

"Then let me help you!" Scarlett said eagerly, moving close to him. He could smell the ashy tang of the fire in her hair. He breathed it in gratefully. "I have far more time. Get me the logs and *I* can go through them!"

"It will not be as easy as that. Father *uses* them. If they disappear, he will know-" Gabriel was suddenly cut off, as a loud, piercing howl cut through the air and screams erupted in the square.

10-SCARLETT

Dawn was breaking when Scarlett and Gabriel ran into the square. "Was that-?"

"-WOLF! IT WAS A WOLF!" Lillian, the local dress maker was screeching.

Scarlett and Gabriel ran over, dodging the townsfolk. "What?" Scarlett gasped, glancing quickly at Gabriel. "That is not possible! My mother wiped them all out!"

"What happened?" Gabriel asked as people rushed around in a panic.

"She was attacked," she sobbed, as a bloodied body was carried up the stairs of the tavern, followed by several healers.

"Where is my mother?" Scarlett demanded to know. Lillian pointed towards the fires. "Mother!"

Scarlett ran to her. "I want you home immediately," Ingrid said flatly, throwing a quiver of arrows over her shoulder.

"No."

Ingrid froze, turning back to Scarlett. "Excuse me?"

"I said *no*, Mother," Scarlett repeated defiantly. "I am helping you."

"You most certainly are *not!*"

"THEN WHY TRAIN AT ALL? You said you wanted me to be able to depend on myself, Mother! To stand on my own two feet. Now is the time to let me."

Ingrid looked down. "Vera has been attacked, Scarlett. I cannot have it be you next time," she said quietly.

"Vera?" Gabriel gasped, looking back to the tavern. "Where is the baby?"

"Genevieve is fine, Gabriel," Ingrid said coldly. "And Vera will be too. The healers will make sure-"

"-I WARNED YOU!" a coarse voice screamed across the square. "I WARNED YOU ALL!"

"Not *now*, Blue!" Jacques snapped. The old man hobbled down the tavern stairs and into the square.

"NO, THIS IS EXACTLY THE TIME! THAT WAS *NOT* A WOLF! NONE OF THEM EVER WERE!" The townsfolk became quiet.

Scarlett stepped forward. "What do you mean, Blue?"

"Pay him no mind, Lass, he is old and crazy!" Rohan called.

"That is what you said ten years ago, but I was right *then* and I am right *now!*" he insisted.

"I am listening, Blue," Scarlett said softly. "Tell me."

When he spoke again his voice was quiet, but shaky. "They were not wolves, but *Weres*. Wolf form they can only carry during the nights of the full moon, but during the day they walk tall… as man."

"You see! It is nonsense! Weres indeed!" a woman cried out.

"Hush!" Scarlett kept her eyes locked on Blue's. She nodded.

"I tried to tell them all, but they *would not listen!* The attacks on the livestock? They started on the first night of the full moon and lasted three nights. The following month, people started being taken," he went on feverishly. "People started reporting more and more wolf attacks, but only ever at night, and *only ever at the full moon!* Nobody noticed this but me, and nobody noticed that, at first, it was the *same wolf* committing the attacks. Only *after* the first people were taken during that second month did people start reporting seeing other wolves!"

"Because they were not wolves," Scarlett finished. "They were Weres, turning for their first full moon."

"Yes! It makes sense!" Gabriel gasped in shock. "I have been going through the death records from the plague! All the deaths *were* in three day blocks, then weeks of peace before they started again!"

"Are you suggesting that someone actively *planned* to terrorise Boque?' Jacques asked. "That one Were created hundreds of others simply to prey on us?"

"I am not suggesting it at all," Blue answered coolly. "I am saying it outright. One Were started all of this." He nodded sadly. "I tried to explain to Vera…"

"Vera!" Scarlett gasped. "She will turn?"

"NO!" Ingrid snapped, stomping over to Blue, stopping less than a foot from his face. "THIS IS IMPOSSIBLE! If what you say is true then *every wolf I slew-*"

"-Was human," Blue finished.

"My *husband?*" she whispered, tears in her eyes.

Scarlett held her mother, her eyes welling also. "What of Vera?"

"It is only the first night of the full moon… She will turn tomorrow," Blue confirmed, nodding.

"Surely you are not suggesting that tomorrow she will turn into a wolf and start attacking us all?" a man yelled. Angry shouts started in the crowd.

"NOT IF WE TAKE PRECAUTIONS!" Blue bellowed back, silencing them. "Weres are more animalistic, yes, but that *does not mean* they have lost their humanity!"

"Then why was it necessary to kill them all during the plague? They were attacking in droves once their numbers became too great!" Jensen reminded him. "Surely you are not suggesting we grant them mercy? If Vera is to become one of them, she places us all at risk!"

"They were dangerous because they were newly turned," Blue told him. "On a Were's first full moon, the primal drives are fresh and raw. It is then that the bloodlust is at its greatest. It is then that whoever orchestrated the wolf plague would release them all to prey on the town. We lock Vera down when she turns tomorrow night and the night after. We make sure she cannot escape or hurt herself, and when she turns at the next full moon, in one month from now, you will see that she is different," Blue insisted. "She will be calmer, more of her own mind. We have always been a loyal town. We *cannot* simply disregard her now when she needs us the most, and Genevieve deserves to know her mother."

"Genevieve's *mother* is no more if what you say is true!" a woman yelled angrily. "She is a *monster!* We should end the risk while we have the chance!" The angry mutterings began again.

Ingrid was steadily collecting herself. "Definitely not! Vera is one of our own and she has hurt *no one*. We will protect her as we would anyone else." She turned around to face the crowd behind her. "THE PRIORITY REMAINS

THE SAME AS IT WAS DURING THE PLAGUE!" she rallied, raising her voice.

"What is that?" Grace asked softly, but still easily heard, as the crackling of the fires was the only sound that remained in the otherwise silent square.

Ingrid returned to the fire and collected her bow. "Find the Alpha."

11-GABRIEL

Gabriel searched with the people of Boque all day for the wolf; the Werewolf, if you believed Blue. Scarlett, Ingrid, and Aunt Grace were all in the same group with him, all of them with countless weapons from the storage shed; all hand selected by Blue. "Silver, Gabriel," he had said softly. "It is not a well-known thing that Weres cannot abide silver. They tend to keep it to themselves."

"Then how is it that you know?" Gabriel had asked.

"I am a very old man, Gabriel," he had responded.

They thought they had the best chance of finding the wolf while it slept during the day, deep in a den in the forest, but as much as they searched all the haunts Ingrid had found during her hunting days, again and again they left empty handed.

"It will be out again tonight," Jensen grumbled. "We have to return to the village and prepare our houses."

"I need to go and check on Hector," Aunt Grace sighed. "The drunk old fool is probably starving at home without me after how much he drank last night." She placed her bow over her shoulder. "Good afternoon everybody!"

"Stay safe, Grace," Ingrid embraced her warmly, before she took the worn path leading home. "Be sure to be within the wall before nightfall!"

"I will see you all home," Gabriel said, staying by Scarlett. She smiled at him.

"We will not be going home, Lad," Ingrid told him. "We go to prepare Vera for the night."

♠

Vera was bandaged down the left side of her body, from neck to thigh. She was pale, but alive.

"It will take more than a Were to take down a mother of Boque!" the healer Janus barked harshly. He was stooped with age, but sharp as a tack, and there was not a single person in Boque you would want healing you more than he. People had often joked that he was actually a necromancer; every lost cause, every rabid fever, every shattered limb; he healed them all with a gentle touch and a rough voice.

"What are the plans for this evening?" Ingrid asked as Scarlett held baby Genevieve up for her mother to see.

Blue came out of the shadows of the kitchen. "Janus believes he has just the thing," he said. "I think we should go old fashioned and use chains and a locked cellar, but he is adamant it will work."

"That what will work?" Ingrid pressed.

"A tonic," Janus said with a wink. "A *sleeping* tonic; the strongest I have."

"Will that work?" Gabriel asked, shocked at the idea.

"Weres are animals, just like humans are," he explained slowly. "I have tested my tonic on horses to be sure of the dosage. We put Vera to sleep before the sun sets; with her wounds, a good long sleep will do her good. Then, we see for ourselves about this Were business and all being true, the town will be safe as she sleeps through till morn."

"And what if you give her too much?" Jonathon asked, his face red and blotchy. He would not take his eyes off his wife.

"I promise you, I will only give her a small dose. Only once she changes, *if* she changes and starts to stir will I give her more," Janus promised. Jonathon nodded.

They were interrupted by the door banging open and Aunt Grace rushing inside. "Gabriel!"

He quickly followed her outside, Ingrid at his heels. "Is everything alright? What has happened?" Ingrid asked, taking Aunt Grace's hands in her own.

"I-I went home to find Hector," she stammered. "He was not in the h-house. I searched everywhere!"

"Aunt Grace, Father could be anywhere," Gabriel told her gently. "There is nothing to fear. He more than likely woke up and came looking for us."

"N-no, that is not why…" she stuttered. "I came in the door and looked through the house. I could not find him, so I went to check the stables and…"

"What is it? What happened?" Gabriel pressed.

"Birch was gone… and in the m-mud by the stable doors … were *paw prints*." Aunt Grace almost squeaked, holding her hands to her face. "Huge things! Our *feasting platters* are smaller!"

Gabriel's heart sank into his boots. "Father…" He turned to Scarlett, looking back and forth erratically. "I know he has done horrible things-"

"-He is one of our own," Ingrid cut him off, no emotion in her voice. "We will find him."

Gratitude flooded into Gabriel; he felt tears spring to his eyes. "But… but we have been looking all day and did not find *anything*. If he was out there, surely we would have found him while we searched?"

"Not necessarily," Ingrid answered. "We were searching the woods. Hector is an intelligent man. If he saw the wolf coming, he easily could have evaded it and ended up anywhere."

"Then where do we look?" Gabriel asked frustratedly, the tears starting to fall.

Ingrid stepped forward and placed a hand on his shoulder. "We don't, Son... We lock down the village for the night. We start the search in the morning. If your father is alive, he will remain so for the night. If he is not, it will do no good going looking for him and leaving Boque at risk."

Gabriel blinked away the tears, nodding, but still stung by the suggestion that his father may be dead already and they should not look for him. "Where do we start?"

Ingrid nodded her approval. "Good man."

♠

Boque's fortifications had been solidified. It had taken all afternoon to finalise what the townsfolk had started while they were away hunting during the day, but they were confident it was enough to keep the Werewolf out.

It was impossible to protect the outer farms, where they were completely open to the fields and forests beyond, but the main town, inner square and most houses and businesses fell inside the wall that they were able to effectively build up and monitor by creating guard stations and shifts for watches that would run all night. Those in the outer farms were coming in and being housed by closer living citizens. No one would be alone. It would not be possible for anything to get in without being noticed.

Gabriel felt relieved at how well the village was protected. With his father potentially lost, nothing would bring Gabriel closer to complete destruction than if something happened to Scarlett also.

He did a final lap of the perimeter, before heading towards the tavern, which would be the basis of operation for the evening patrol shifts and where Vera was to be housed for her first turning. He was riding Ash, who, thankfully, had still been in town when the paw prints had appeared at his stable at home.

"Nothing like this has been seen since the plague," Aunt Grace had said.

When he had completed his circle, he found himself back at the main gates. Ingrid was giving instructions to Jensen, who would be guarding the main gates with Rohan and Jacques for the first shift. Gabriel made a decision. "I am going back to the farm," he announced, trotting over on Ash.

Ingrid's head whipped around so quickly Gabriel was worried she had hurt her neck. "What? Absolutely *not!* We need you here to help guard Vera. She has already been bound and put to sleep with Janus' tonic. There are to be six guards *at all times*. We cannot afford to have you off gallivanting around!"

"I have to, Ingrid," Gabriel said, shaking his head. "I have to look for my father one last time. If he is there, he has no idea we are fortifying the town and I need to bring him back," he explained. "If he is not there, I will return immediately. You have my word."

Ingrid looked pensive. She breathed deeply, turning to face the forests. "Sunset is an hour away," she said softly.

"I will be back," Gabriel assured her. He tapped Ash's side and rode through the gates. "I promise!" he called back over his shoulder.

He galloped at full speed all the way to the homestead, leaving Ash right at the foot of the stairs and flying up them with an almost inhuman speed. "FATHER!" he yelled once inside the door.

Silence.

Gabriel tore through the homestead, searching it room by room. He had checked the entire upper storey before running back downstairs when he heard it; coughing. He ran down the hallway to the bathroom, and when he burst through the door, his father was slumped over the edge of the large steel tub. "Father! Where have you been?" he cried out, rushing to Hector's side. "Did the wolf attack you? It did not bite you, did it?"

"Bite me?" His father was breathing heavily. His arms and chest had grazes that had partially healed. The bath water was pink with lost blood. He coughed again. "The… the wolf. It was here," he began to explain slowly. "The grazes came from the forest." Gabriel picked up a rag and started cleaning off his father's arms. "I got too drunk… did not want to make an arse of myself like… like last time. I thought it best to come home." He paused, a hand over his eyes. "I was locking up the stable when I saw it. I managed to get away on Birch-"

"-Birch is alright?" Gabriel cut in.

Hector nodded, before stopping and starting to shake his head. "No… No, Boy. I lost him in the forest. He hit a hole and went down. I had to leave him behind." Gabriel felt a stab in his heart. "His loss may very well be the only reason I survived."

"Father, I have to tell you," Gabriel said to him. "It is not a wolf." Hector looked up, his dark eyes weary. "It is a Werewolf. That is why I asked about bites."

Hector's eyebrows shot to his hairline. "What?"

"It is true Father. I studied the death records from the plague myself. They always came at the full moon-"

"-You have been listening to Blue, you have," his father cut him off.

Gabriel paused. "H-he explained it to the town after you left last night. Father, there was an attack. It got Vera! People thought he was crazy, but it all makes sense! Boque is being readied as we speak. We *have* to be inside the gates before sunset!"

Hector paused for a moment, apparently deep in thought. Then he shook himself. "Yes, Boy. Yes! Get me up, quick!" He started to pull himself up. "Where is the towel? Very good- Ready my axes! We must leave as soon as possible!"

12-SCARLETT

Scarlett was stroking Vera's hair as Janus replaced her bandages. She was lying on a stretcher, being readied for the evening. She was to be strapped down, then placed in the locked cellar of the tavern once the tonic had taken effect. Guards would be placed at every entrance. "Looking good, my Dear! There is a little oozing, but with any wild animal bite or scratch, that is to be expected. The balms will do their job and you will be just fine," he was telling her.

Vera just stared off to the side, to her daughter's bassinet, where baby Genevieve lay sleeping. "I am going to turn into a monster, aren't I?" she whispered softly.

"Vera," Scarlett said to her. "Whatever happens, whether it be changing into a wolf or nothing at all, you are Mrs Vera Hardwick, wife to Jonathon and mother to Genevieve. What you are does not matter so much as *who* you are."

Tears rolled down her cheeks as Janus readied the tonic. "Scarlett," she said hoarsely. "You have to promise me something."

"What is it?"

"That if the worst should happen…"

"I promise you, the town will make sure Jonathon and Genevieve are taken care of."

"Thank you," she choked back a sob. "But if this is truly happening… promise me, promise me that you will not let me live like this. Tell them-*force* them if you have to… but make sure they kill me."

Scarlett gasped in shock. "Never!" she hissed. "You have a husband and child and they deserve to know you! I will *not* have you speaking this way!"

"The last thing they deserve is to have me afflicted, placing them at risk every day of their lives."

"Vera," a voice came through the front door. It was Blue. "You cannot think this way," he told her, closing the door behind him. "Many Weres have lived long, healthy lives. You are a mother of Boque; borne a child this very month. If you can handle that, you can handle this ten times over," he said to her gently. "Two nights. Two nights of your entire life are going to be trying. You can do this. Unlike the Weres of the past, you are not alone." Tears fell from her eyes, rolling down her face, past her temples and into her hair as she looked at Blue from her place on the stretcher.

Janus approached delicately, holding a measure of the tonic. "Are you ready, my Dear?"

Vera looked fearful, but nodded. He handed her the tonic and she drank it in several gulps, then she handed the cup back to Janus. "What if it is not enough? How will you get me to take more if I wake up?"

"These," he answered, lifting up a dart from the side table. Vera's eyes widened. "Do not fear. The tonic is thinned to the consistency of blood. It is shot using a blow pipe- or can be used by hand if you are close enough." He pointed to the needle tip. "It will pierce your skin and inject the tonic directly into your bloodstream. It means no one has to risk themselves getting too close and it will act more swiftly than ingesting it."

"That will hurt, will it not?" she asked fearfully. She looked to Jonathon, who had crossed from Genevieve's bassinet to his wife's side, taking her hand in his.

"Darling," Blue said softly. "Weres are incredibly strong creatures, and the adrenaline you will be feeling at your first turning will likely mean you will feel nothing at all, especially if it is used while you are stirring, and anything you *do* feel, you will even more likely never remember," he went on, reassuring her. Vera's breath was coming in short gasps and her eyes had welled up again, but she nodded quickly.

"Talk to us, Vera," Scarlett said.

"I am… scared," she answered. "I can feel the tonic in my body. It is getting… hard… to…" Her eyes fluttered closed and her head dropped to the side.

Jonathon dipped his forehead to hers, kissing her softly and stepping back. "What is to happen now?" he asked shakily.

"We turn her," Blue said, directing Janus to Vera's other side. "Onto her side." Jonathon looked confused. "When she turns-" Jonathon flinched. "-she will be a wolf. When we bind her, this positioning will ensure that she is comfortable. Hopefully, this will also aid in keeping her asleep."

The binding took almost an hour. Once Vera was in the correct position, Blue had Scarlett bind her feet and hands together. "We need them tied gently here, Scarlett," he told her. "Too loose and she will escape; too tight and the binding will break when she turns." As Scarlett tied her limbs, Janus tied the straps across her body, binding her to the stretcher on which she lay. "Now, the chains," Blue directed. Jonathon insisted on doing this himself. "Should she wake up, which hopefully the tonic will prevent her from doing, these bindings will only delay her. She *will* escape them eventually."

"You only tell us this *now?*" Jonathon exclaimed.

"Yes," Blue answered. "I would see her be given the opportunity to come through the other side of this. If I had said this before, the town may have stolen and done away with her by now to save the trouble," he said. Jonathon scowled. Scarlett could see his underlying pain.

"This makes the cellar fortifications all the more important, as they will be the second to last line of defence should she wake, after the guards. The stretcher will go into the boiler room of the tavern," Blue instructed. "There, she will be warm, but it also has steel framework. We have the best possible chance of keeping her in there. We take her down and expunge the fires so there is no chance of her burning herself or acting out of fear of the flames should she wake. Then, we barricade the door to the stairs," he finished.

"Are you sure of this, Blue?" Scarlett asked for possibly the twentieth time.

"No," he answered simply. "Have I come across Weres in my time; yes. Are they all the same; definitely not. The Were that planned and executed this plague is the darkest creature I have seen in all my years. To cultivate packs only to use them as fodder for the town; to create the illusion of a plague to effectively build one, and for what? Until we find out who the Alpha is that started all of this, we will never know the true intent behind their actions."

He turned to the sleeping Vera. "She is kind and good, and once she passes her first full moon, she will be again, *that* I can assure you," he said to Jonathon. "A Were is the same person they were before they were turned. You will have your wife again." Jonathon teared up again, sniffing. "Thirty six hours…We just have to get her through the next thirty six hours. If I had my way I would pull down the stairs completely in the boiler room so she was unable to reach the door at all, but Hellah would not hear it."

Jonathon breathed deeply, before going to the door and calling in the townsfolk who would be guarding Vera. In walked Jensen, Jacques, Ukara, Renni and Martok. Ukara and Renni worked at the mill, while Martok was a cattle farmer. He had valiantly released his hundred head of lovingly cared for longhorns. "If the town should fall once again to a wolf plague, they are lost anyway, and should they lure that monster in so we can kill it, or keep it distracted long enough feeding it loses interest in us, then all the better," he had explained. Martok was a good man.

The men crossed to Vera with Jonathon and together, they carefully lifted the stretcher. Scarlett held her breath until they had left Janus' cottage, then turned back to him and Blue. "Will you be alright with Genevieve?"

"I birthed her, didn't I?" Janus snapped. "The babe will be just fine with me, Girly. Go on and find your mother."

"I will be taking my leave," Blue said quickly, making for the door. "I need to lock down my house."

"Thank you, Janus," Scarlett answered, following Blue out into the failing sunshine. The sun had had just reached the top of the trees on its way down. Scarlett set off to find Gabriel, but the closest she found was his Aunt Grace. "Grace! Have you seen Gabriel?" she asked.

"Y-yes, Dear," she answered, fear in her eyes. "He… he returned to the farm to look for Hector."

"What?" Scarlett gasped. "No! He will be trapped out there!" She began to whip herself into a frenzy. Hector had done horrible things. It was wrong of her to have assigned blame for them to Gabriel when he was innocent in the matter. If something happened to him; if she never had another chance to make it up to him and tell him how she felt, it would be the greatest regret of her life.

She took off down a laneway, heading to the weapons store. "Scarlett, wait!" Scarlett barely heard her. At the weapons store she pulled out a full kit; a sword and sheath at her waist, a dagger strapped to her ankle and a quiver across her back.

She was almost finished, when Keenen appeared on the other side of the store. "Scarlett, what are you doing?" he asked.

"Going to find Gabriel," she answered flatly, pilfering through the store. "He is outside the gates."

"Listen, you cannot leave," he began, panicked. He was pale and sweating, despite the winter air. "I need to talk to you."

"Now is not the time, Keenen. If it is important it can wait until morning," Scarlett told him dismissively as she searched for the bow that matched her quiver.

"No, Scarlett! I mean it, you *cannot* leave Boque!"

"Keenen that is *enough!*" she snapped. "I will *not* be marrying you and you have *no* power over me! Now leave me be, I am busy!" Once the bow was in her hands, she headed to the main gates, leaving Keenen at the weapons store. When she arrived, she was immediately waylaid by her mother.

"Where do you think *you* are going?" Ingrid demanded.

"I am going to find Gabriel," Scarlett told her. "I cannot leave him out there."

"This was *his* choice! And you will be just as reckless as he if you leave!"

"Mother, the *sun is setting!*" Scarlett cried out desperately.

"Exactly! You must stay *here* where you are s-"

"-They are coming!" a voice called out from the top of the gates. It was Daynar, the silversmith. His shop had been cleared of its delicate weapons for use against the wolf.

Ingrid snapped to attention. "Wolves?" she yelled back.

"Hector and Gabriel!"

Scarlett gasped and exhaled in relief. Ingrid nodded, moving towards the gates. "THESE GATES GET CLOSED AND BARRICADED THE SECOND THEY ARE INSIDE! WE HAVEN'T A MOMENT TO LOSE!" After two excruciating minutes, Gabriel and Hector, who were atop Ash, came through the gates. "READY? AND HEAVE!"

As the gates closed, desperately slowly, Scarlett ran to Gabriel, who had dismounted Ash. She threw herself into his arms. He chuckled softly, holding her tightly until she pulled back. "Are you alright? How could you leave like that? You did not even *tell* me? What if you hadn't made it back in time?"

Gabriel allowed her to continue as long she had more to say, and when she had finally exhausted her arguments, he pulled her close again. "I am here. Both my father and I are safe, and we are going to see this night through; I promise," he whispered as he held her.

Scarlett blinked back the tears of angry frustration that had sprung to her eyes during her tirade. When she looked passed Gabriel to Hector, she saw he looked angry. "Hector," she said. "I am glad you are safe."

Hector gave a swift nod. "I will be checking in with perimeter guards," he told Gabriel. "Find somewhere to bunker down and *stay off the streets*," he said gruffly as he climbed down from Ash and handed the reins to Gabriel.

"But Father, I wish to help!" he protested.

"NO!" Hector roared. "You will go and care for the children in one of the houses if you want to do something of worth, but I expect you to do the same for yourself," he commanded. "We will argue about it in the morning when this night is over." Then he headed down the path that led to the tavern and the eastern edge of town.

"He is not wrong," Gabriel said to Scarlett, looking her in the eyes. "The more protection the children have, the better."

Scarlett laced her fingers through his, meeting his gaze unwaveringly. Then she moved forward and planted a gentle kiss on the side of his mouth. "I will be wherever you are," she said, squeezing his hand. Gabriel grinned and squeezed back.

They followed the same path Hector had taken, but when they reached the tavern, they turned right and headed for the western part of the town. It was the furthest from the forests and the houses there were made of stone rather than wood, far safer for protecting the children of Boque from attack.

They were just passing the leather maker's tanning cottage when they heard a rustling sound coming from the alley. "What was that?" Gabriel asked.

Scarlett took a step back and looked down the alley. The shadows were getting longer and she could not see all the way down. "Hello?" she called out. She felt a sense of ominous déjà vu, flashing back to that afternoon in the woods when she was ten.

"Scarlett," a disembodied voice called back.

Scarlett paused, relief flooding her. "Keenen? Is that you?" Keenen stepped out of the shadows. His face looked haunted.

"Scarlett you have to help me," he said.

"What is going on, Keenen? You have been behaving strangely all afternoon!"

"You do not understand!" he hissed desperately, his hands in his hair. "I *saw* it!"

"You saw wh-*you saw the Werewolf?*" Scarlett gasped.

"Wait, you know who it is?" Gabriel exclaimed, coming forward. "And you haven't *said* anything?"

At seeing Gabriel, Keenen paled further and stumbled backwards. "Get away from me!"

"Keenen? We are not going to hurt you?" Scarlett said to him, but Keenen stumbled backwards in an attempt to get away. In the instant he threw his hands up to shield his face, like he was protecting himself from a blow, Scarlett saw it; a deep gash wrapped around his left forearm. She gasped. "Keenen!"

He was gone. He took off running down the back alleys behind the tanning cottage, where a group of clotheslines stood with the purpose of drying the leather after the tanning process. Scarlett tried to follow him, Gabriel close behind her, but by the time they reached the other side of the clotheslines, he had completely disappeared.

"Scarlett, we have to find him. He *knows* something!" Gabriel suddenly paled. He was looking past her. When she spun around she saw two things. One was that the last rays of the sun had disappeared below the horizon... the other was a large grey wolf almost filling the opening between two houses.

As they stared, it began to howl.

The sun had set.

13-SCARLETT

"Run!" Gabriel hissed. Scarlett took off through the tanning leathers, her hand in his. They changed their direction as often as they dared. Behind them, the howl continued. Ahead of them they could hear yelling from the town streets.

Scarlett felt her cloak tighten around her neck and she was pulled backwards, landing flat on her back amongst the drying leather. "SCARLETT!" Gabriel yelled, rushing back to her.

Her cloak had gotten caught on one of the clotheslines. She ripped at the clasp and let Gabriel lift her up, just as another howl sounded to their right. They had just managed to jump out of the way when the light grey beast tore through the cloak

"We have to get to a house!" Scarlett cried out as they ran.

"I do not think we will make it!" Gabriel gasped as he ran, his breath coming in short bursts. They speed through the alleys and hit the main street. A single arrow flew past Scarlett's ear and she stopped short.

"STOP, THAT'S MY DAUGHTER!" Ingrid screamed from the head of a throng of people in front of her. Every able bodied citizen was armed with the silver weapons from Daynar's shop.

Scarlett and Gabriel ran forward. "IT IS RIGHT BEHIND US!" she yelled.

With another howl, the wolf leapt from the shadows and onto the street, snarling and growling. 'READY YOUR WEAPONS!" Ingrid commanded to the crowd.

Scarlett and Gabriel joined the line of people. "Ingrid, have you seen my father?" Gabriel asked.

"He is with the northern border patrol," she answered as the wolf started running full pelt at the crowd with no hint of fear. "AIM CAREFULLY! F-!" Ingrid was unable to get the word out, for as she went to order the assault, another figure leapt forward and hit the grey wolf square in the chest. "ANOTHER WOLF, STAND YOUR GROUND!" she bellowed. "TO MY LEFT AIM FOR THE LIGHT GREY; TO MY RIGHT AIM FOR THE DARK!"

The wolves snapped and snarled back and forth, but as much as the light grey tried, it could not dominate the newcomer, who was twice as large and clearly much older given the silver stripes in its fur. There was a high yelp as the older wolf's jaws locked onto the paw of the younger and Scarlett watched as it fell back.

It was not giving up however, as she saw it get back to its feet and leap at the older, larger wolf, which lowered itself to the ground as though to pounce. When the light grey wolf was about to land, the dark grey launched itself up and knocked it down. The younger hit the street in a puff of dirt and the crowd watched as the older wolf stalked over to it, placing a paw on its neck as it growled deeply. After a few whimpers, the light grey wolf grew still. The dark grey turned to the crowd.

"Ready yourselves!" Ingrid said in a low voice. The archers raised their bows and the townspeople behind them readied their swords.

"Wait!" Scarlett stepped forward. Gabriel grabbed her arm.

"Scarlett, get back here!" her mother hissed. The crowd would not attack without her mother's order. In front of them all, the dark grey wolf emitted a high pitched whine, before settling onto the ground and placing its head on its paws.

Scarlett turned to Gabriel. She stepped forward and kissed him softly. "Trust me," she whispered. Gabriel looked fearful, but he nodded and let go of her arm.

Scarlett walked towards the giant, dark grey beast. "Scarlett!" her mother called again.

The wolf whimpered, not moving. Scarlett moved steadily closer, until she was right in front of it. "Are you a Were?" she asked softly. It whimpered again, raising its head off its paws.

Scarlett stepped back; another whimper. She came forward again, watching the creature closely, the crowd behind her silent. She looked at its eyes, and gasped when she recognised them. "Blue?" The wolf got to its feet. "Blue?" Scarlett said again, stepping closer. "Is that you?"

The wolf came up to her shoulder in height, larger than any she had seen in her life, whether in stories, dreams, or reality. It came forward, stopping by her side. Then it put its head down. Scarlett placed her hand on its head between its ears. The fur was thick and coarse. She shuddered at the feeling, flashing back to the ten year old who was attacked at her grandmother's.

When she came back to herself, she laughed, dropping to her knees and taking Blue's wolf face in her hands. "It *is* you!" Blue gave a short bark.

"Impossible!" Ingrid gasped, suddenly at her side with Gabriel.

"He told us so himself! Weres are not all the same," Scarlett said delightedly. "And now he has saved us! Thank you Blue."

Blue began to whimper again, going back to the light grey wolf and pulling on its paw, trying to drag it away. "What is the matter, Blue? Do you want us to move him?"

"He is telling us that the danger is far from over," Rohan said, coming forward. "That is not the wolf that attacked Vera last night," he declared. "It is the wrong colour."

"You mean there is *another* one?" Gabriel exclaimed. Blue whimpered again, still pulling at the paw of the other wolf.

Scarlett went to Blue and placed her hand on the younger wolf's side. "It is still alive!" she cried out, feeling a faint heartbeat. "Someone help me!" She turned back to Blue. "Is he a Were too? Turned last night?" Blue dropped his head slightly.

"We have to get him locked up if this is his first full moon," Rohan said, heaving the wolf off the ground and placing him across his shoulders. "I think we can just about consider Blue's word gospel now!" He turned to Blue. "Where do we take him?" Blue trotted off down the street. "Lead the way," he huffed, following.

Scarlett turned back to the crowd. "The wolf that attacked last night is still a threat!" Ingrid was saying. "Back to patrol everyone."

"Mother!" Ingrid turned to her. "I am going to follow Rohan and Blue then go and check on Vera to see if she has woken."

Ingrid paused, considering her words. Then she nodded. "Scarlett?"

"Yes, Mother?"

"You have done me very proud tonight." Scarlett smiled, then took Gabriel's hand and followed Rohan.

They met him at the grain store cellar, where Blue had led him. He had lowered the light grey wolf to the ground to open the cellar doors.

"Let me help you," Gabriel offered, moving forward and lifting the lower end of the wolf while Rohan took the front, its head draped around his neck. Blue led the way down the stairs and into the cellar. Scarlett was last in line.

When she reached the bottom of the stairs Gabriel and Rohan were gently lowering the still unconscious wolf to the floor. They stepped back and Blue came forward, lying beside him and placing his head on his paws.

"You are going to stay?" Rohan asked. Blue jutted his head forward slightly. "Alright, you have certainly proven you can handle him should he wake."

The small group ascended the stairs and chained the doors closed on the other side, before placing sand bags over the top as a barricade. "I am going to check on Vera," Scarlett told the men.

Rohan nodded. "I will come with you," Gabriel declared. "Rohan, are you coming? Jacques is on patrol there; you can check in?"

"No, Son," Rohan answered. "I trust you will keep them all updated. I am going to check the perimeter patrols and report back to Ingrid. The more we keep our information up to date, the better."

"If you see my father-?"

"-I will tell him to find you at the tavern," Rohan answered, before he strode off towards the perimeter wall to the west.

At the tavern, Vera had yet to stir, but the men on guard listened with rapturous attention. "Blue?" Jensen gasped. "Blue was one of them all along-?"

"-He was completely lucid? Not aggressive at all-?"

"-He *knew* you-?"

"-He took down another wolf-?"

"-He was adamant Vera would be alright if she made it through this full moon," Jonathon said. "This is how he knows." He looked as happy with the news as he could be, given the circumstances. "We just have to get through tonight… and tomorrow!"

"She can do it, Jonathon," Scarlett reassured him.

"This is wonderful news," Ukara said. "The best we could have hoped for! If Blue was able to grapple with the other wolf and subdue it then he could do so again with Vera if she wakes!"

"Hopefully, we can avoid that," Gabriel said. "We do not know if the other wolf, whoever it is, will survive, and if we need Blue for Vera and the other wolf wakes while he is here-"

"-We will be right back to where we started," Renni finished.

"Someone should go and guard the grain store. We need eyes and ears on it at least," Ukara said.

"I will go," Jensen offered. "Martok?" Martok nodded.

"What about the guard here?" Jonathon protested. "We cannot be two men down!"

"Gabriel and I will stay," Scarlett told him. "We will watch the interior door in their absence." Jonathon exhaled in relief and nodded.

Gabriel opened the door for Scarlett and they crossed the threshold into the tavern. It was significantly warmer inside. Scarlett placed her bow on the table. She had lost the quiver when she had torn her cloak.

In the far corner, where the door to the boiler room was, stood eight colossal wine and mead casks. "If Blue could take down that other wolf as easily as he did, surely Vera will not be able to get through that full of Janus' tonic." Scarlett said.

"I would not count her out," Gabriel said, hanging his cloak on the hook. "For all we know the other wolf is a child. It looked a lot smaller than Blue."

Scarlett had not considered that. Blue had been reluctant to harm the light grey wolf, and without eyes on Vera, no one knew how big she was after having turned. Scarlett collapsed into a chair.

"How are you feeling?" Gabriel asked, taking a seat beside her.

Scarlett sighed. "It is a lot to take in. The wolf plague was orchestrated by a Werewolf and no one knows why. They were not wolves at all, but more Weres," she continued. "Your father used that as a means to kill my father and so, court my mother. Blue was a Werewolf all along," she stopped thoughtfully. "And we still have another one out there that started the whole thing. It is a lot to learn in such a short period of time... and I still feel like there is something we are missing!" she finished.

Gabriel stood up and pulled her out of the chair, putting his arms around her. "Scarlett," he began softly. "I promise you that we will see the other side of this." He lifted her face to meet his in a tender kiss. She felt her body melt into his arms. When their lips parted, he gazed into her deep brown eyes. "I love you, Scarlett."

Scarlett's heart began to race, blood rushing through her ears and down her body. "I love you too," she whispered. Their lips met again; the kisses heavy and forceful; passionate. Gabriel's hands grasped her hips firmly, as his lips left hers and went to her cheek, before moving down her neck.

Scarlett pulled at the buttons of his shirt, until it fell away completely. Gabriel pulled away long enough to move his hands to her face, brushing away the strands of hair falling across her eyes before moving to kiss her again. Her tongue darted across his lips, enticing him deeper, as her hands travelled down his bare chest to the corded belt of his pants.

Scarlett could feel his growing bulge in her hands, and Gabriel moaned softly into her mouth as she grasped him firmly. He then pushed her back onto the table behind her and took hold of her hips again, before sliding his hands upward, removing her shirt and exposing her breasts. Gabriel kissed his way down her chest, teasing her erect nipples as he moved down.

When he reached her navel, Gabriel began to work his way back up, every kiss sending an electric shock up Scarlett's spine. She could feel herself growing wet with anticipation as her groin began to throb almost painfully. As Gabriel worked his way back towards her breasts, her breathing coming heavy, his hands worked at the buckles of her pants.

Scarlett was still grasping and rubbing against his hardening package, she too, pulling at his belt buckle. She slid his pants down, exposing his manhood to her for the first time in waking reality. Scarlett gasped as Gabriel pushed forward, pressing the thick shaft up against her as he kissed her again.

She pushed him back, leaving Gabriel standing alone in his nakedness, before she kicked off her boots and removed the remainder of her pants, joining him. Then she reached forward and placed one hand behind his neck, the other back on his hard member, drawing him back to her.

Gabriel dropped down and wrapped his arms around her hips, kissing her breasts as he lifted her onto the table. Then, as Gabriel gasped at her touch once more, Scarlett drew him into her. As he plunged deep inside, his erect length filled her completely, bringing with it warmth that travelled steadily up her body, Scarlett let out a low moan and closed her eyes.

Gabriel drew back slightly then thrust forward. Scarlett's eyes flew open at the impact and her head fell backwards. As it took over her fully and completely, she lost all sense of the world outside her body, but she could still hear when Gabriel's breathing started coming short and sharp. She could hear when he moaned loudly as he moved. With every thrust Scarlett was barely able to catch her breath before the next one came.

Then she was. Waves upon waves of energy coursed through her body in an explosion of pleasure filled bursts. Gabriel was with her wholly and utterly. Scarlett could feel her legs becoming slick with their combined juices as his member pulsated inside her and his thrusts became slower.

When it finally came to a stop and Scarlett could feel her brain begin to work again, she lay back on the table, her bare chest still heaving as she fought to breathe. Gabriel lay down on top of her, his head nestled to her chest. Scarlett wrapped her arms around his head and ran her fingers through his hair, her legs still wrapped around his waist. Such relief her body felt from the release, that when Scarlett fell asleep, she had nothing to dream about.

14-GABRIEL

The growling began in the early hours of the morning. Gabriel and Scarlett had extricated themselves from each other and dressed as rapidly as they could the moment it started, but Ukara was faster. His eyes widened as he deliberately looked away, keeping his eyes firmly on the open tavern door.

"Has Vera broken her bonds?" Scarlett asked.

"She is waking," he informed them quickly. He then went and alerted the outer door guards. One took off to alert the other patrols.

"Any news?" Gabriel asked, standing between Ukara and Scarlett.

"Uh... One of the wolves in the grain store cellar has started to scratch at the door, but no one is willing to open the barricade because they cannot tell if it is Blue or... or the other one," Ukara stammered.

"I can," Scarlett declared, coming forward.

"Are you sure?"

"Absolutely. Come and guard in the interior door. Dawn is close and so far, she is only just stirring. It is bound to take her a while to fully wake from the tonic." He nodded and replaced her and Gabriel inside so they could go to the grain store.

They found Jensen staring disconcertedly at the cellar doors on their arrival, the barking and scratching sounding insistent and agitated. "Is all well, Jensen?"

"I do not know," he answered, not taking his eyes off the door. "I could not risk opening the doors without knowing for sure."

"Have you heard any other sounds besides the scratching and barking? No growls or snarling?"

"No."

"Open the doors," Scarlett ordered. "Quickly! If Blue needs to get out it must be for a reason." The three moved as rapidly as possible to get the doors open. The moment they were, Blue came leaping out and took off down a side street, heading towards the town square.

"BLUE!" Scarlett called, dashing after him.

"Stay here and keep an eye on the other one!" Gabriel called to Martok, tossing him his silver sword before sprinting after Blue and Scarlett.

He had to check both ways when he hit the main road to see which way they went. To the right was a patrol crew roving the western border. To the left, in the distance, he could see Scarlett running towards the village square, her dark hair billowing out behind her. He took off after her as fast as his feet and lungs would allow.

He caught up to Scarlett as she cried out in alarm, the moment they reached the square. Blue was growling; a deep, menacing sound that carried throughout the entire square. On the other side of the main fire, pacing back and forth, was another wolf. It had long black fur and talons that glinted in the moonlight.

"How have we gone from no wolves to *four* in one day?" Ingrid growled, coming up behind them, her bow at the ready.

"Is that it?" Gabriel asked. "The one that attacked Vera?"

Ingrid nodded an affirmative. "Where is your sword?"

"I left it with Martok. He is guarding the other wolf."

There was no time to ask after Scarlett's. At that moment Blue leapt at the black wolf, tackling it to the ground. The attack was brutally vicious, with each wolf ripping and tearing at the other, wherever they could reach. The black wolf was a ruthless savage, at one point tearing off the last four inches of Blue's tail. He yelped in such a high octave it rattled Gabriel's ears; his blood splattered across the courtyard, but even then Blue did not relent.

Again and again the wolves came at each other. It seemed they would never stop, until the moment came when the both of them faltered, stumbling on their front paws. They caught themselves in exactly the same manner, before looking to the sky.

Then, the black wolf turned and bolted into the rapidly disappearing shadows as the first light of dawn turned the sky a charcoal grey. "AFTER IT!" Ingrid roared, pulling herself onto Storm and galloping away, closely followed by her patrol crew.

Scarlett had run to Blue, whose body was twisting and contorting as they watched. "Scarlett," Gabriel said softly. "Come away." She allowed him to pull her back, but would not move more than a few feet away.

Blue's fur receded into his body, leaving bare, pale, bloodied skin behind. His muscles lost their tension and form, returning to that of an elderly man. Scarlett rushed forward, pulling off her cloak, and placing it over the top of him. "Thank you, Girl," he said quietly. "It is greatly appreciated. I do not know what would have become of me if you had not intervened last night."

"I could say the same. I have spent many years being hunted by wolves; in life and in my dreams," Scarlett answered. "I was not about to let the kind acts of one go unacknowledged. You saved us, and by subduing the other wolf-"

"-THE BOY!" Blue suddenly roared, getting to his feet and heading towards the grain store. "He will have woken!"

"It is a boy?" Gabriel asked as they followed him down the street.

"Yes!" he called back, Gabriel and Scarlett half running to keep up. "We need to get him to Janus. I have not fought as a Werewolf in a long time... I did not quite know my own strength!"

"You need to see Janus too! You are injured!" Scarlett exclaimed.

"Blue!" Gabriel called to him as they ran. "Do you know who it is?"

"He smelled familiar," Blue answered. "But scent works differently as a wolf. I could not place it."

They made to cross the main street that ran through the heart of Boque and head down the lane that led to the grain store, but Gabriel saw something that made his heart stop and his body freeze. "What is it?" Scarlett asked, slowing her pace but not stopping. Blue continued on. "Gabriel, come *on*, we have to go!" she pressed.

"Look," he said, pointing. Scarlett glanced up and inhaled sharply.

Vera.

She was sitting out in the sunshine, the early morning light dancing across her face as she smiled at her daughter, who cooed happily in her arms. Jonathon sat beside her, tears of joy still running down his face. Gabriel and Scarlett ran over, stopping short before they hit the young family.

"Vera!" Scarlett cried out, throwing her arms around her. "You are alright!"

Vera laughed. "Yes! I am."

"Do you remember anything after going to sleep?" Gabriel asked her.

Vera's face grew thoughtful. "Dreams," she answered. "Fierce; sharp; nothing specific. Mainly I felt... things; hunger and longing. I could tell that I wanted to wake very badly."

"You were human when you awoke?" Scarlett went on.

"I believe so... When I came into my mind and could think clearly again, I was me at the very least."

"How are you feeling?"

"Better than ever!" she laughed again. "My body feels slow. Janus says it is the lingering effects of the tonic, but my wounds have *completely* healed!"

"Incredible!" Gabriel gasped. "How is that possible! Blue was injured last night and he was still hurt after he turned back?"

"Turned back?"

"Vera, my love," Jonathon said softly, holding her shoulder. "Blue is a Werewolf too. It is how he knew… how we could take care of you, and how he knows you will be yourself again after tonight."

Vera paled at the thought of another night. "Blue is a Werewolf also?" She paused, fear crossing her face. "Was it he who…who-?"

"-It was not he who attacked you, Vera," Scarlett assured her.

"How can you know for sure?"

"He saved us all twice last night, as a wolf. His fur is a dark grey with white patches. He fought another newly turned wolf. It had light grey fur. The other had black fur," Gabriel explained.

"It was the black wolf who attacked me," Vera told them in barely a whisper, as the sound of hoof beats steadily filled the air.

"We know. Whoever it is attacked someone else the same night as you. Blue fought them both off last night," Jonathon said.

"We lost it! Whoever it is will be human again by now. We lost them!" Ingrid announced, climbing down from Storm. "Vera! Dear girl, you look wonderful! How are you?"

"I am very well indeed, Ingrid. Thank you," she answered. "You were tracking the wolves?"

"Wolf," Ingrid corrected. "The brute that attacked you, but now he is injured," she said with a relish as she loosened Storm's saddle and removed her bag, slinging it over her shoulder. "The moment we find him, we will know."

"There is another, Gabriel says?"

"Yes. Someone was attacked when you were. They changed last night as soon as the sun went down," Ingrid's voice became quiet. "If it was not for Blue he may have killed us all."

"Who is it?" she asked.

"Let us go find out, shall we?" Ingrid suggested to Gabriel and Scarlett. They bid goodbye to the Hardwicks and made their way to the grain store cellar, where Ukara and Renni were inside, clearing away a split bag. "How is the damage?"

"A lot better than it could have been," Renni answered, frowning.

"Where is the boy?" Gabriel asked. "Is he alive?"

Ukara scoffed. "Yes... Yes, he is alive."

"Did they take him to Janus?" Scarlett asked. The men nodded in unison.

Janus' home was surrounded by people, all of whom were murmuring quietly to the people around them. When they walked among them, the crowd parted respectfully so the group could pass through.

Janus stood before them, his back turned as he bent over the body on his table. Blue, his clothes replaced, was on the other side of the table talking to whoever it was that lay on it. "You are strong, Lad," he was whispering. "Broken bones, while painful, will mend. What you cannot do is give up the sanctity of your mind. If you lose yourself, all is lost. You may as well have died, for you will become the very animal you fear you are."

A quiet sobbing was coming from the corner of the kitchen. Scarlett clutched at Gabriel's hand and squeezed. When he looked at her, she had a look of horror on her face. He followed her gaze toward the crying figures in the kitchen.

It was Rohan and Jacques, and on the table… Keenen.

15-SCARLETT

Scarlett could not get past her shock at seeing Keenen on the table. She stood there staring, Gabriel at her side, while her mother crossed the room to console Rohan and Jacques. When Janus stepped back, Keenen was revealed, his face and the small amount of exposed skin bruised and swollen. That which could not be seen was covered in a multitude of bandages. Most of his torso, both arms, his full left leg and almost all of his right were wrapped in tight white cloth. He seemed to be sleeping, but it looked as though he had been prepared for burial.

"Alright old man, your turn," Janus barked at Blue. Scarlett took Janus' place beside Keenen as he walked around the table to see to Blue's wounds. Blue did not argue, but refused to leave Keenen's side.

"Will he… I mean, is he going to…?" Scarlett started.

"He has a lot of broken bones," Janus said. "He may not be able to breathe well under exertion with the damage to his neck and throat in the future. As to whether he will survive, that lies with him, I am afraid."

"What do you mean?" Scarlett asked.

"His body is torn, but not unrepairable," Blue explained, wincing as Janus began to clean and stitch his wounds. "Were's bodies are incredibly resilient, but he was babbling incoherently when I got to him in the grain store cellar, and he was in such pain that when he would try to move he would start screaming," he looked down, shamed. "Once he was here Janus put him under so he could examine him properly; fix him up. There is no way of knowing if his mind is whole, or if it has been torn asunder by the ordeal."

"He saw who attacked him and Vera," Gabriel announced to the cottage. It immediately fell silent; Janus pausing his work. "He knows who the black Werewolf is."

"Well, he will not be able to tell you before tonight, let me tell you!" Janus said loudly, returning to Blue's shoulder. "I do not expect him to wake until at least tomorrow, maybe longer, and even when he does, there is no way of knowing what he will remember, if anything at all! You cannot place your bets on this one, I am afraid," he exhaled sharply. "You will have to find the answer somewhere else."

"And that we will!" Ingrid said. "Blue, you gave him pause, that other wolf. Wherever he is hiding, he could not have gotten far. We will find him before the sun sets this time. He cannot possibly hide all day. He will need to seek help or die from his injuries!" She turned to Jacques and Rohan. "He does not have Janus seeing to him like Keenen does." They nodded, their breaths coming out sharply as they fought to keep the tears back.

Gabriel had a sudden thought. Could it be? Could he really find the answers there? He made for the door. "Where are you going?" Ingrid called after him.

"The farm," he answered, not pausing in his stride as he made his way down the front steps.

"Wait!" Scarlett said. "I am coming with you!" Gabriel paused long enough to turn back to Ingrid.

"What do you think you will find there?" she asked.

"Hopefully…" Gabriel replied. "Answers."

They turned to leave. "Wait, Scarlett?" She turned back to her mother questioningly. Ingrid dug into the bag at her hip.

Scarlett's mouth dropped open. Her mother was pulling out a long, red cloak. "Mother! Why-?"

"-Because the other one was ruined and it is *winter*, Scarlett," Ingrid answered practically, holding it out to her. "And because it is time you claimed the image… Make it your own rather than one others have thrust upon you."

Scarlett slowly reached out and took the cloak, pulling it over her shoulders and doing up the clasp. It was a snarling wolf head. "Grandmother and her ironic humour."

Ingrid smiled. "It suits you." Scarlett returned her smile.

Getting to the farm took longer than expected, as his father still had Ash. The sun had well and truly risen by the time they came through the front door. "Where are they?" Scarlett asked the moment they were inside, knowing why Gabriel had to return without him ever having to tell her.

"Study!" he called back to her, taking the stairs three at a time until he reached the second storey landing. Scarlett matched his pace easily. "Here!" he grabbed several books from the shelves, passing a large red one to Scarlett. "This is the log from the final years of the wolf plague. It names every death; cause, time and date."

"Alright?"

Gabriel then gave her a small book with large fold out pages. Instead of words, it had a five by seven box grid with circles in each; a moon calendar. "Start with the full moon of the first month. Confirm the wolf attacks only fall on the three days of the full moon."

She nodded and started diligently checking the deaths and dates against the moon calendar. Gabriel pulled out his father's work log and started analysing the patrol crews his father had set up, checking the crew lists against the moon calendar. Each entry had the crew list, what area they were monitoring, any works undertaken, kill numbers, and any injuries. "The Werewolf *has* to be a part of father's crew, how else could it stay informed about where the patrols were to avoid them this long?" he was saying. "We should be able to narrow down the list of potential names based on who was not on patrol during the full moon."

The work was tedious, but Gabriel steadily checked every single crew entry in Hector's work logs, every tree lopped, every wolf slaughtered, every injury sustained, creating a list of names on a blank notepad on the desk. "Oh, your father had four kills in one night," he said conversationally. "Also logs an injury for him."

"What kind of injury?" Scarlett asked with interest, taking the book. "'Superficial cuts; wrapped up on location, minimal damage'," she read. "I think I remember that."

The work continued. Occasionally Scarlett would interject. "Frederick died a year or so later. He is not alive anymore," or "It cannot be Yula, Gabriel; I saw him with mother last night." And so the list was first created and then slowly whittled down.

"Scarlett?" Gabriel suddenly said. "There were eleven men lost the night your father was injured?"

Scarlett confirmed the date and checked the matching work log. "Yes," she confirmed. "Eleven deaths recorded in the patrol and one person taken as they locked away their sheep."

"That was the last night of the full moon?"

"Yes, why?"

"The following month, the first night of the full moon; how many deaths?"

Scarlett checked the death log. "Almost ten times more than the month before!" she gasped. "Oh… here is my father…" she whispered. Gabriel came around the table and held her as she breathed heavily into his arms. "I am alright," she insisted, drawing away. "So… so the Werewolf specifically targeted people to turn, and the rise in deaths the following month is linked to the influx of newly turned Weres?"

"It looks like it," Gabriel answered, and they both came to look at the list Gabriel had compiled. Seven names.

"Wait, Kallum also was a part of your father's crews and not on any of the full moon lists. Why have you not included him on here?" Scarlett asked.

"He was on patrol those nights, just not as a crew member. He was patrol leader." His stomach then loudly announced its lack of sustenance with a growl worthy of

Blue. "Let us go and get something to eat, then we will take the list to your mother."

Downstairs Gabriel pulled out the remaining bread, cheese, and jerky from the pantry as Scarlett started a fire in the grate. When the cheese had melted across the bread and the jerky had disappeared, Scarlett got to her feet. "I am going to use the bathroom before we leave."

Gabriel nodded. He had been holding himself far too long also. He was considering just how impressive the human body was, to shut down its functions when faced with danger or issues of higher importance, when he heard Scarlett scream.

Gabriel leapt to his feet and raced to the hallway, but Scarlett was already at the entrance. "The… the bathroom!" she stuttered, clearly terrified. Gabriel was there in three steps.

The other side of the door looked like the back room of a slaughterhouse. Blood covered the floor in pools and splatters, some specks trailing up the walls. Tufts of fur trailed in balls across the wreckage of the room. The smell seeped into Gabriel's nostrils and he gagged, almost bringing up his lunch.

"Gabriel," Scarlett said in a small voice behind him. He did not turn around, frozen in his shock and panic.

"Gabriel!" she said more insistently. "We have to go and tell my mother!"

"What could she possibly do?" Gabriel's brain was foggy and slow. He needed a plan; he needed to *think*, but he could not.

"Gabriel," Scarlett repeated. "Do you not understand what you are seeing?"

"Of course I do!" he yelled in pain and desperation. "My father is gone!"

Scarlett came forward and held his face in both hands, forcing his eyes to meet hers. "Gabriel… why was Kallum patrol leader during the full moons?" she asked quietly.

Gabriel was thrown by the question. What did that have to do with anything *now*? Kallum had been cleared! "What?"

"Kallum was patrol leader during the full moons," Scarlett said again, very slowly. "Every single one. *Where was your father?*"

All at once dozens of memories came to Gabriel, his mind snapping back to crisp and clear, every synapse firing. His father with blood on his hands; coming home with fresh meat even during the coldest winters despite the butchery being empty; the work trips that always lasted *exactly* three days; never fearing the woods, day or night; never losing his way, even in the worst storms; how ravenously he would eat before he left for his trips and when he returned; his responsibility for Scarlett's father's death. No, he *caused* her father's death. He stumbled back out of Scarlett's hands. "No... no, no, no!"

"Gabriel! It is going to be alright, I promise!" Scarlett said loudly. She grabbed his hands. "But we *have* to go and warn everyone!"

Gabriel nodded, moving toward the door. Cloaks in hand they ran back to Boque as fast as they could, not stopping to rest until they reached the main gates. "Daynar!" Scarlett called up to the lookout platform. "Have you seen my mother?"

"She was making her rounds last I saw her, Lass!" he called down to them. "I would check the tavern!"

They ran on, heading for the town square, on the edge of which stood the tavern, stopping everyone they met. "Get to the tavern! Tell everyone you see! NOW!" The flow of people steadily changed, until all were moving in the direction of the Boque tavern. Gabriel leapt up the stairs and charged through the door. "Father! HAS ANYONE SEEN MY FATHER?"

"Hold up, Lad," Jensen said. "Not since he went on patrol last night. What has happened?"

"Is Mother here?" Scarlett asked.

"I am right here!" Ingrid came out of the crowd and embraced her daughter. "What happened at the homestead?" she asked Gabriel.

"I NEED EVERYBODY LISTENING!" Gabriel yelled into the crowd, climbing up onto a table.

"OI!" Hellah exclaimed in protest at the use of her furniture, as the hubbub of the tavern crowd quietened. The door and windows were open to the square.

"I have come from my home!" Gabriel began. "Scarlett and I have been going over the crew logs for the wolf patrols during the plague and compared them to the death logs!" he explained. "My father's patrol crews were almost identical every single full moon, including the fact that Kallum was patrol leader for those three nights *every month!*"

"You are not accusing me, are you?" a voice cried out in shock. The crowd parted and up walked Kallum himself, pushing his way through the bodies.

"No, Kallum," Gabriel told him. "I do not accuse you, but tell everyone here… Why were you patrol leader instead of my father?"

Kallum looked thoughtful. "Well, I was his second in command!" he said finally. "I would always cover for him when he was on trips to other towns!"

"*Every single full moon?*" Gabriel pressed meaningfully.

Kallum looked shocked, then confused, then angry. "Are you publicly accusing your *father-?*"

"-I was attacked on the first night of a full moon," Scarlett cut him off. "A night that *you* were patrol leader and Hector was apparently away on business. If that were so... how could he have saved Grandmother and myself?" she asked.

Kallum looked stunned. "He... he said he returned home early and heard the attack as he passed," he said softly.

"WHEN I RETURNED HOME FOR THE LOGS, BLOOD AND FUR COVERED THE BATHROOM!" Gabriel told the crowd, his voice carrying all the way to those listening outside. "IT WAS THE SAME BLACK FUR AS THE WOLF BLUE FOUGHT LAST NIGHT!" He lowered his voice again. "If I am wrong, I will spend the rest of my life making amends to him, but Werewolf or not, he is clearly hurt. There is no other way so much blood could have appeared at the homestead otherwise."

The crowd murmured uncomfortably. Ingrid climbed up beside him. "THE EVIDENCE IS BEFORE US!" she boomed. "HECTOR WILL BE GIVEN FAIR CHANCE TO DEFEND HIMSELF, BUT HE *MUST* BE FOUND! SPREAD OUT AND FIND HIM! NO ONE GOES ANYWHERE UNARMED! *NO ONE* GOES ANYWHERE ALONE!"

16-GABRIEL

Ingrid formed a search party and immediately took them into the forests, dividing teams into quadrants to search to dense woodland. "Jensen, lead your team to the south east and come back through the eastern gate; Martok, head out the south gate and move to the west. My group will exit through the main gates with Jensen and move south," she instructed. "Move swiftly, but quietly. Pay attention to any trails of blood or damaged greenery. Move out!"

Scarlett watched as her mother left through the town gates, then followed Gabriel to Janus' to check on Keenen and Blue. If they could not find Hector before the sun set, Blue had to know what he was up against.

Both of them were asleep when he arrived with Scarlett. "How are they?" Scarlett asked Janus, keeping her voice low.

"Blue is just resting before the sun goes down," he answered gruffly. "He is sore, but he will be fine."

"And Keenen?"

"Until he wakes we will not know how his psyche has held up. We can only hope he gains his strength and does not wake until he is ready for the world again."

Scarlett nodded. There was a low stirring moan and then Blue was rising from the cot by the fireplace. "What word?" he grumbled.

"Blue!" Scarlett exclaimed softly. "The other Werewolf, we think it might be Hector!" she told him quickly.

"What?" Janus started.

"How could you know this?" Blue asked.

"There was blood and fur at home," Gabriel told him. "We spent hours combing the woodcutting and patrol logs and father was *always away* during the full moon! It cannot be a coincidence."

"But he *saved* me during a full moon, so he was not really away on business!" Scarlett added.

Blue furrowed his brow in thought. When he started talking, his voice was quiet and slow. "I spent many years as a wild Werewolf, before finally settling here as a young man. I roamed for years after I was turned, plucking the odd chicken or grouse when I was not able to find anything on the hunt.

"I settled here, convinced that I could earn enough to satiate me during the full moon and I would be of no harm to anyone. I took the apprenticeship at the slaughterhouse, where I had access to everything I could possibly need.

"It has been a good life, but I have sought to keep to myself… never marrying or bearing children… fearing my affliction could be passed on or that I would harm them somehow."

"But you have never hurt anyone!" Scarlett protested.

"Have I not?" he said sadly, gazing at Keenen.

"That is not the same, Blue!" Gabriel insisted. "You saved us all!"

"And if it means the death of your father?" he asked. "Will you feel the same then?"

Gabriel fell quiet. Scarlett slipped her hand into his and squeezed. "He killed your father," he whispered to her, his throat tight.

Tears appeared in Scarlett's eyes at the thought. In the moments he remembered the facts, a relationship with Scarlett seemed impossible. Then, his eyes would meet hers and all doubt would be stripped from his mind. Nothing would keep Scarlett from him, especially not the man who had already created a plague to torment Boque and had robbed Scarlett of her father.

Gabriel looked back to Blue. "Family is more than blood," Gabriel said. "I cannot protect my father from what he has done… and I will not."

♠

"Thank you Blue," Jonathon was saying. "We will be repaying you all the years of your life for what you have done for us."

"You can repay me by taking the time to learn what it means to be a Were," he answered matter of factly. He took Vera's hand. "Now, my Dear, you have one night to get through. Like last night, you will be handling it alone. If I had my way, I would be there to guide you, but with the black wolf still out there, my duty must be to the town as a whole."

"The tonic worked last night. I am sure it will do so again," Vera told him.

"Not necessarily. You will be much stronger than last night. The first months of a Werewolf's life is filled with monumental growth. Janus will need to double the tonic and even then... I will be surprised if it works," Blue continued. "If it does, your metabolism will burn it off quickly. It most certainly will not last all night."

Vera seemed scared, looking from Genevieve to Jonathon. "What do I do?" she asked fearfully.

"All we can do is what we did last night, with the amendments to the tonic. I would suggest introducing silver, but in such a young wolf we would run the risk of killing you. I do not want that," he added quickly, as Jonathon made to protest. "We can add more chains for additional protection." Vera did not look assured. "For all we know the black wolf will be found before the sun sets and I will be able to be right here by your side." Blue smiled kindly, before clasping little Genevieve's hand for a moment. "I will return to Janus and inform him of the plans for the tonic.

"Thank you, Blue," Jonathon said as the three left the Hardwick home.

Outside, people were running back and forth. "What is going on?" Scarlett asked Jeda, Geri's blacksmithing apprentice.

"They found Hector!" she trilled, her high pitched voice ringing through the air, before she saw Gabriel standing there too. "Oh! I-I am sor-"

"-Where?" Blue asked.

"At the edge of town, near the east gates."

"Go back to the forge, Jeda," Gabriel said, not unkindly. "Stay safe."

"Yes, Sir!" she piped, and took off towards the black-smith.

Gabriel led the way to the eastern edge of town, but when they arrived, the area was eerily quiet. "Where is everyone?"

"Does not seem like the place a rogue wolf was found, to be sure," Blue said, sniffing the air. "But he has definitely been here."

"Could the smell not be from last night?"

"It could have been, but he headed west after our fight. Unless he was on this side of town when he turned... *before* I confronted him in the square... his scent would not be here."

Gabriel paused. "Can... can you follow it?"

"I am not a dog, Boy," he growled back.

"I know... I just th-I am sorry." Gabriel fell silent.

"Relax, Lad. If he is close... I will find him." Blue took the lead, Gabriel and Scarlett backing away as to not taint the scent. He led them down and around the back of the mill, towards the southern gate. Before they reached it, Blue turned off again, almost completing a full loop of the mill, but turning off at the last second. Two more turns later, Blue froze. "No... it *cannot* be!"

"What is it, Blue?" Gabriel asked.

"Janus!" Scarlett gasped. They were standing in the backyard of the healer's cottage. "Blue?"

"He is here," he answered softly. Gabriel could hear shouts and rumbling coming from inside.

"Blue, stay here," Gabriel told him quickly, running for the door.

"Are you daft, Boy?" he snapped. "Sunset is within the hour!"

"Exactly. If he turns, the element of surprise will work in our favour."

Blue looked down. "I do not like this."

"I promise, Blue," Gabriel said. "We will call at the first sign of trouble."

"And I will hear you," he answered.

Gabriel and Scarlett crept up the stairs as quietly as they could, before slipping silently through the door. The fireplace was ablaze. Ingrid and group of Boque citizens surrounded a chair that stood before it. Chained to the chair, was his father, torn and bloodied, but smiling.

"Father!" The group turned to Gabriel and Scarlett.

"Hello Gabriel," he answered, his voice sickeningly sweet. "Be a good boy and unlock the chains, will you?"

"Gabriel, you should leave," Rohan told him.

"He is my father."

"He *attacked* my son!"

"And Vera," another voice pointed out.

"And I deserve answers just as much as you do!" Gabriel insisted.

"ENOUGH!" Ingrid commanded. "Gabriel is right. Let him stay." Rohan stepped aside and allowed Gabriel and Scarlett to enter. They passed through the group to Ingrid's side, where Aunt Grace was looking on fearfully, tears running down her face.

"We found him in the forest," Ingrid told them, never taking her eyes off him. "He tried to outpace us... his wounds did not make it easy." She stepped forward. "Hector Juvan Bloom, you are before us standing accused of murder, attempted murder, conspiracy, inciting a plague and sedition. What have you to say?"

"I say you have no proof, and the onus of responsibility is on you to share it when you state your claim," he spat.

"We have your work logs from the plague. We have your admission witnessed by myself, my daughter, Mason and your own sister and son... We have fur and blood found at your home, matching the wolf in question."

His face contorted with rage. "YOU SEARCHED MY PROPERTY WITHOUT CAUSE!"

"WE SEARCHED NOTHING!" Ingrid roared back. "Gabriel and Scarlett reported the find. Grace willingly allowed us in to confirm. As your heirs they have the right to allow such a search in your absence.

"Where were you, Hector? If you were not hiding your wounds from the people who would recognise them for what they were, what were you doing?"

"Searching the woods for the beast, *where you found me!*"

"Where is Janus?" Scarlett suddenly asked. "He could easily confirm where the wounds came from."

Ingrid shook her head. "He is preparing Vera for the night ahead."

Jensen came forward. "You have heard the accusations, Hector. You have heard our evidence. How do you plead?"

Gabriel watched his father, sitting there silently. Ingrid lost control of herself, coming at him aggressively. "YOU CREATED COUNTLESS WEREWOLVES FOR YOUR PATROLS TO KILL TO EXHALT YOURSELF IN BOQUE! YOU ORCHESTRATED THE DEATHS OF HUNDREDS OF PEOPLE, MANY OF YOUR OWN WORKMEN TO BOLSTER YOUR BUSINESS FOR FINANCIAL GAIN! YOU ALLOWED NEWLY TURNED WERES TO ROAM UNSAFELY, LEAVING MY MOTHER AND DAUGHTER OPEN TO ATTACK! CREATURES WHO MAY NEVER HAVE HURT ANYONE IN ALL THEIR YEARS HAD THEY SURVIVED THEIR FIRST FULL MOON! AND I

UNKNOWINGLY KILLED INNOCENT PEOPLE BECAUSE OF IT! *INCLUDING MY HUSBAND!*" Ingrid struck him in the face; once, twice; before she could strike him again Rohan restrained her, Grace coming forward to place her arms on Ingrid's shoulders, Scarlett holding her hand at her side.

Gabriel watched on in horror as his father began to laugh. "You did not kill your husband, Ingrid." His smile grew. "...I did!"

"What?" Scarlett exclaimed. "You kept track of every wolf you turned so you could kill my father yourself?" she yelled.

"No... not every wolf," he said slowly. "I saw Spiro that night. Full moon... It would be his first. The sun hadn't quite gone down. He told me he was feeling sick, so I took him to his dear mother in law's cabin in the woods; the closest house to his patrol... coincidentally." He chuckled, throwing his head back to get his hair out of his eyes. "Told him I had something that could help... dosed him with some of Janus' tonic. The very same that is being given to Vera right now. An unconscious mind cannot turn, you see?

"Rosa had him settle nicely into her bed; Scarlett was already asleep by the fire, exhausted from her trip through the woods… then I waited for dawn. New Weres take longer to turn. Those used to it can do it faster; easier," he smirked.

"The tonic wore off just before dawn, as planned. Spiro woke and attacked… and the moment the sun rose I was there… to finish him before he could turn back," he finished, looking out the window, seemingly unfazed. Gabriel was stunned by the confession, and the silence that followed told him the other townsfolk were in a similar state.

"You?" Ingrid said, her breathing becoming heavy. "You set my mother and daughter up to be attacked… so you could *kill my husband?*"

"He orchestrated the attack on you and your grandmother so he could save you and play the hero," Gabriel whispered.

"Th-the logs!" Scarlet trembled. "They recorded injuries… There was only one the last night of the full moon the previous month… Father."

"Why, Hector?" his Aunt Grace sobbed into her dress. "Why tell us this now? For repentance? They will surely hang you for this!"

Gabriel's heart ached knowing what was to come and how painful it would be for his aunt. His father looked at her, disgust on his face. "Why, you ask, *Sister?*" He rose from his chair, the chains falling away. How long had he been faking being bound? Ingrid drew her sword. "Because now… you are too late," he said, looking satisfied.

Gabriel spun to look outside… just as the final rays of the afternoon disappeared and darkness descended on Boque.

17-SCARLETT

"BLUE!" Scarlett screamed, bolting for the door. "EVERYBODY OUT NOW!" There was a stampede for the door as fur and fangs violently exploded from Hector's skin. Scarlett lost sight of Gabriel as she grabbed her mother and followed Jensen and Martok out the door and into the yard. Blue was waiting, the silver in his charcoal grey fur shimmering in the moonlight that lit up the entire town.

Hector appeared at the doorway, growling deeply. Blue growled back, unrelenting. Hector leapt from the top of the stairs to the bottom, lowering his head and slowly stalking Blue's movements.

Suddenly, he shot off to the left, coming straight for Scarlett's mother. "NO!" she screamed, as Ingrid froze in shock.

"FATHER STOP!" Gabriel bellowed, appearing at Scarlett's side and throwing himself in front of her mother.

Blue was faster. He charged at Hector, leaping on his back and clamping onto the back of his neck. Hector let out an ear shattering howl of pain and threw himself backwards in an attempt to throw Blue off. They both hit the ground, blood dripping from Hector's neck and Blue's tail, as well as the wounds they had gained the night before.

Hector snapped at Blue's legs as they both struggled to get to their feet, their progress hindered by the unwavering attacks. Scarlett watched in horror as Hector gained the upper hand long enough to claw his talons across Blue's chest. Blue fell back and Hector took the opportunity to get to his feet, coming barrelling in Scarlett's direction.

Instead of attacking her however, Hector disappeared into the darkness of the Boque alleyways. Blue was up and after him in an instant. "AFTER THEM!" Rohan roared, charging after the wolves.

"Go and find Janus!" Ingrid yelled, following Rohan. "Get the tonic darts!"

Scarlett nodded and raced off with Gabriel at her side. They were at the tavern in minutes. Janus was just coming down the stairs. "Janus! Is Vera alright?"

"Sleeping like Genevieve!" he answered brightly. "What's ruffled your feathers?"

"Father and Blue are fighting again!" Gabriel told him. Vera's guards on the cellar door exclaimed in shock.

"They are somewhere in the city! We need the tonic darts!" Scarlett puffed.

Janus cursed, fumbling with his bag. After far too many agonising moments, he pulled out several darts and a blow pipe. "Sorry about your house!" Scarlett yelled as they ran back to the centre of town.

"WHAT ABOUT MY HOUSE?" Janus bellowed after them.

When they reached the town square, they stopped and listened. The sounds of the howls and barks could be heard in the distance, but with the echoing nature of the valley, it was hard to tell where it was coming from.

"What do we do?" Scarlett asked helplessly.

"We either split up to search or stay here and wait and let them come to us," Gabriel answered.

"We cannot split up. There is only one blow pipe."

Gabriel kissed her quickly. "Then we look together, because I could not possibly stay still."

Scarlett nodded. "That way," she pointed to the west.

The moon arced high overhead when at last they came across the mob of villagers chasing the warring wolves. "Mother!" Scarlett cried out, gasping for breath.

"Scarlett! Where have you been?" she yelled angrily. "Where is the tonic?"

"Here! I am sorry but we could not find you! The howls sound like they are coming from everywhere!"

"Where are they?" Gabriel asked.

"They disappeared again. We have lost and found them twice already," Aunt Grace said.

"We should go back to the town square," Scarlett suggested. "If they are running all over town, we are more likely to come across them there.

Ingrid agreed. "To the square!" The set of at a steady march, listening to the sounds of the howls in the distance.

They had barely gone a hundred feet when Renni came flying out from between the houses. "SOMEONE HELP!" he screamed. "IT IS VERA! VERA IS WAKING!"

"OH NO!" Gabriel and Scarlett looked at each other. "The tonic!"

"Blue never got to tell Janus to double the dose!" They started sprinting towards the tavern. The howls grew louder and sharper. They were close. Scarlett came out into the town square and she could see, at the very end, Hector and Blue continuing their battle. "You get the blowpipe to the fight! I will get a dart to Vera!"

Gabriel nodded and followed the crowd down the street, while Scarlett ran after Renni, tonic dart in hand. "She started stirring at midnight, now she is awake. We do not think she has managed to break out of her chains yet."

Scarlett nodded. "Where is Jonathon?"

"Inside."

Scarlett entered to find Jonathon staring at the casks, muttering under her breath. "What is she doing?"

"Jonathon? Are you alright?"

He did not take his face off the casks. "I can hear her tearing the room apart. She has broken her bonds."

"Blue was worried this would happen, but we were waylaid before he could tell Janus to double the tonic dose!" Scarlett explained, showing him the dart. "We have to get this in her quickly!"

"How could he have been so careless?" Jonathon yelled angrily.

"Hector was found. Blue went to intercept him. I am so sorry, but I promise you, we will do all we can for Vera, even if it means me going in there myself."

Jonathon blinked back tears, then nodded. "What do we do?"

"Find a way to get me in there. The casks will take too long to move."

"The cellar door? Outside?"

Scarlett nodded quickly. "Stay here!" She ran out into the night to the cellar door, where Renni and Ukara were on guard. "We need to unchain the doors!"

"What?" Renni gasped.

"Are you insane?" Ukara snapped.

Scarlett held up the dart. "I have to get this into Vera before she hurts herself or someone else. That door will not hold long." Ukara and Renni looked torn. Behind her, the fight between Blue and Hector had spilled into the square proper. Scarlett turned back to see Hector snap at Blue's leg. "Hurry! Or there will be three Werewolves to deal with!"

Ukara and Renni began shifting the sand bags, while Scarlett pulled at the chains around the handles. The wolves behind her grew louder, the snarling so loud it hurt her ears.

She turned to watch. Blue was weakening, but she could see splatters of blood forming under Hector. "We need to end this," she whispered. She looked down at her hands, to the tonic dart. After a deep breath, she let if fall from her fingers.

As the men removed the last of the sand bags, Scarlett opened the doors. "Stand back," she said to Renni and Ukara, and she backed away from the entrance, as far into the square as she could. Then she whistled.

A deep growl escaped the tavern boiler room, before a flash of white fur exploded into the night. Vera had short fur, with light brown patches down her back. The moment she landed, she braced her stance, threw her head back and howled.

The reaction in the town square was immediate. Both Blue and Hector froze, turning to the newcomer. Vera stalked into the square, growling deeply as she regarded them both.

Hector growled back, but Blue ran forward, keeping low to the ground before launching himself at her, tearing at her right ear. The fight exploded immediately, Vera snapping back at Blue and Hector leaping into the fray.

"Why did Blue attack Vera?" Scarlett whispered to herself. "He had to know it was her?"

The mauling continued, as each wolf bit and snapped at the others, until Blue barged Hector and he went skidding across the icy street. He then turned to Vera and raised himself up to his full height, growling fiercely. Vera growled back, but dropped her head slightly.

Blue turned back to Hector, Vera behind him. Then the two of them began to circle. Hector backed away, growling. When they got too close, Hector howled, but both Vera and Blue did not break their pacing, circling him in closer and closer.

Blue made a sudden snap at Hector, who rounded on him and snarled. This took Hector's attention just long enough for Vera to strike. Though much smaller than he, Hector was outnumbered, and with Vera on his back and

Blue at his throat, he had no opportunity to defend himself. He was brought to the ground as Vera ripped and tore at his back.

Blue disengaged and gave a single bark. Vera leapt off and came to stand at his side, but continued to snarl at the people she passed. He turned, growling low as he went, and Vera followed behind him, Blue growling again every time she tried to change route. He led her down through the cellar doors of the tavern and immediately, Renni and Ukara moved to lock them back up.

The townsfolk unfroze from their panic of watching the wolves; a tonic dart zipping through the air and sticking deep into Hector's furry hide. Scarlett ran through the crowd to the other side of the square, where Gabriel waited with her mother and Grace.

"Scarlett!" Ingrid gasped, pulling her into her arms. "You are safe!"

"What happened with Vera?" Gabriel asked. "You were not able to put her back to sleep?"

"I... I did not try," Scarlett admitted. "I let Vera out."

"What?" Ingrid exclaimed. "What were you thinking?"

"Vera was going to break out anyway! I thought it would provide enough distraction for Blue to get the upper hand."

"And if she had attacked you first?" Gabriel asked.

"Then I would have trained under Blue to follow him as my Alpha just as Vera does now," she answered bluntly, holding her head up and looking him directly in the eye.

Gabriel shook his head slightly, before looking to his father, still lying on the cobblestones of the town square. Scarlett saw his eyes begin to well. "I am so sorry, Gabriel."

He nodded, blinking back the tears. "I know," he choked. "But Boque is safe now. That is what matters."

"Unless Vera should escape again!" Grace interjected. She took Gabriel's elbow. "Come, Gabriel. We should see your father to Janus."

Gabriel met Scarlett's eyes. She nodded encouragingly. "Take as long as you need," she whispered. He placed his hand over Grace's and led her toward Janus' cottage, as several Boque citizens carried Hector's body before them.

18-GABRIEL

The walk from the town square to Janus' cottage was the closest his father came to receiving his funeral rites. The sun rose the next morning on a cool, clear winter day. The cellar door that led to the tavern's boiler room was opened and Blue and Vera slowly made their way into the light, squinting.

"I… I escaped," Vera was crying. "D-did I hurt anyone?"

"You protected your pack," Blue answered gently, as Jonathon rushed to her side and pulled her into his arms. "You have done very well, my Dear."

Lillian, the dressmaker and a friend of Vera's who had cared for Genevieve along with the other children of Boque on the western edge of town, returned the baby to her mother, who held her close and sobbed.

The repairs to the town started immediately. The tavern's boiler room had its fire re-lit and its doors and walls repaired. Janus' house was returned to its former glory. The streets were cleaned; the blood washed from the stones. Barricades were pulled down and the gates were opened.

In the afternoon, Janus declared Hector's death and released the body to Gabriel and his Aunt Grace. They took him directly to his assigned plot in the cemetery and Gabriel spent the afternoon digging. Despite the cold of winter, Gabriel was hot and sweating profusely by the time he considered the grave to be deep enough. It was almost twice the size of a standard grave to fit his father's forever body. He insisted on placing it himself, refusing all help as he slid the body into the grave, exactly as the sun set.

As he began to fill in the grave, Scarlett appeared, holding a candle in each hand. Behind her were a line of Boque citizens; Ingrid, Vera and Jonathon Hardwick, Blue, Jensen, Martok, Renni and Ukara; each of them holding a candle.

Ingrid also carried a wolf pelt, which she carried to a grave several rows away and laid over the top. She returned to Gabriel, placing a hand on his shoulder, squeezing slightly for just a moment before going to stand by his Aunt Grace.

"He does not deserve this," Gabriel said, tears in his eyes from the pain and exhaustion. "He does not deserve to be honoured. This is my responsibility."

"We are not here to mourn!" Scarlett said loudly, projecting to the crowd from Gabriel's side. "We are here to support beloved Boque citizens, while they suffer through the pain of their loss." She turned to Gabriel again. "We are here for you, Gabriel, and you, Grace."

Ingrid took a seat with his aunt on the stone benches. He watched Ingrid hand her a candle, then place her now free hand tenderly on Aunt Grace's knee. The tears began to fall. "Thank you," he whispered.

He lifted his shovel and continued on with his task, as every citizen kept a silent vigil, refusing to move or leave until the final shovel of dirt was placed over Hector's body. Scarlett handed him her second candle and together, they stood there one minute more, Scarlett's hand in his, before he was ready to leave. Gabriel leaned forward and stuck the candle into the dirt and held his hand out to Scarlett. She followed suit, placing her candle beside his and taking his hand, before Gabriel led the townsfolk out of the cemetery.

♠

The next day Gabriel returned to the homestead with his aunt, but she could not bring herself to go inside. "I cannot do it, Gabriel," she whispered softly, shaking her head.

"This is our home, Aunt Grace. What will you do if you do not live here with me?"

"I do not know." She suddenly laughed, almost joyfully. "I do not know! But it will be whatever I see fit! I am… free."

Gabriel went in alone. He tidied the living room and went upstairs to place all of the work logs back on the shelves. He was just sitting down to a blank notebook when he heard someone moving around in the kitchen.

He paused at the foot of the stairs and looked around. There was nobody there, but a fire was crackling in the grate, and a cake was sitting on the kitchen bench. "I thought you would like some company," a voice said from behind him. He turned, and standing in the back doorway, an armful of firewood in her hands, was Scarlett.

"What about your mother? What about your home?" Gabriel asked.

Scarlett took the wood to the fireplace and placed them in the iron stacker. Then she stood up and turned to face him. "I am home."

Gabriel rushed to her side and lifted her into the air, kissing her deeply as he slowly lowered her back to the ground. "You will stay with me?"

"Always."

♠

And so, life went on in Boque. Scarlett and Gabriel cleaned out the bathroom. They threw out the old iron bathtub, replacing it with a round pewter one gifted to them both by the blacksmith at Boque's forge. Ash was found at the edge of town, with Martok's cattle. Thankfully, all were well. She and Blaze were made quite comfortable at the homestead's stable, which soon had to be expanded when they discovered Ash would foal in the Autumn.

Keenen woke from his induced coma. He would not leave the bakery for weeks afterwards. Yarraan, Janarri and Victor gave up trying to get him to spend time with them. Rohan and Jacques were growing fearful that their son would never want to see daylight again, when Blue and Vera arrived one morning. Blue carried a book in his hands and Vera carried baby Genevieve.

No one knows what they told him, but soon after Keenen was seen on the streets again. He would smile or maybe even wave to his childhood friends, but he was no longer the same person he was before the attack. Or maybe he was, and he was just now finally allowing that person to shine through without the desire to have a seat at the popular table.

By the time the full moon came around again, Keenen was resolute that he was ready to face it. The town used it as an opportunity, to build relationships; to show solidarity, and so, a tradition was born. The night before every full moon the town would throw a festival, to ensure that Blue, Vera and Keenen had enough food to keep them full over the coming nights.

As news spread of what had occurred in Boque, the town grew into a city. The flimsy wall became a mighty stone barrier and the farms extended to all four corners of the valley, all the way up to the tree line.

Werewolves learned of the haven Boque had become for their kind, and when they began to arrive, Blue would give them the introduction to their city, evaluate their skills and find them a place to call home where they would be valued, or offered a place to develop new skills as apprentices. The children that arrived, he housed himself, with Keenen eventually moving in to help him train the pups.

There were full moons when Vera would not roam with the pack, instead curling up in her home, by the fire, Genevieve snuggled against her white fur. Eventually Blue grew to an age that he maintained the education of the young wolves, but could not roam himself as he once had. He settled into his retirement with Janus, the both of them developing a library of books on lupine care and what it meant to be a Were.

It was when Blue began to focus on the library that he declared Keenen the Alpha of the pack, a responsibility he bore with pride as he grew the pack to become Boque's most valued citizens, for their skills, and their passion for protecting their furless family. He could often be seen on the outer edges of the forest, teaching the younger wolves what wild animals were safe to hunt, or in the town square on market day selling the soft pelts of the animals they had caught while talking to them about the importance of pack life and the safety and security it provided.

Scarlett's nightmares ended, her dreams returning to normal, for no longer did she fear wolves, and no longer did she dwell on her father's death now that her mother had laid what remained of him to rest in the Boque cemetery. She also had no need for dreams to thrill and excite her, for she had Gabriel to do that while her eyes were wide open.

She never replaced the blood red cloak her mother gave her; the one her grandmother had made. After everything she had learned and all she had lived through, her mother was right; the image Boque had bestowed on her was hers to take and change however she saw fit, and there was no longer a single citizen in all of Boque who saw her as a child anymore.

There were no more pitying looks or hushed apologies. There were no sorrowful stares at the scar on her forearm, because with the works she undertook at the farms, hunting with her mother and carving wooden sculptures with all of Gabriel's woodcutting scraps, she had amassed many more.

Gabriel and Scarlett mostly kept to themselves out at the woodcutter's homestead, loving each other tenderly but fiercely day after day... by the fireplace, among the wild-flowers, or deep in the woods in calm, leafy glades... There were, however, occasions when they would return to Scarlett's childhood home to visit her mother, who remained there with Mason and the farming assistants.

One such occasion they snuck inside with a present for Ingrid on her birthday. There was an odd knocking coming from above them. "Mother must be shifting furniture," Scarlett suggested.

"Maybe someone made her a new trunk?" Gabriel shrugged. "I did see Hugo working on something similar when I made a delivery to the carpenter's shop last week?"

They made their way up the stairs and Scarlett reached for the handle of her mother's bedroom door. It made no noise as it swung open, revealing a woman, bare in her nakedness, lying across the bed on her back. On top of her was another woman, trailing her hands along the first woman's breasts as her face was buried deeply between her legs.

Gabriel froze, panicking. His brain ceased to function and from the look on Scarlett's face, so had hers. "Aunt *Grace?*" he gasped.

"*MOTHER?*"